Game On

The Morgan Brothers Series – Book Four

By Avery Gale

© Copyright September 2016 by Avery Gale
ISBN 978-1-944472-33-7
All cover art and logo © Copyright 2016 by Avery Gale
All rights reserved.

The Morgan Brothers® and Avery Gale® are registered trademarks

Cover Design by Jess Buffett
Published by Avery Gale Books

Thank you for respecting the hard work of this author.

This is a work of fiction. Names, places, characters and incidents either are the product of the author's imagination or are used fictitiously and any resemblance to any actual persons, living or dead, organizations, events or locales are entirely coincidental.

No part of this book may be reproduced, stored in a retrieval system, or transmitted by any means without the written permission of the author and publishing company.

WARNING: The unauthorized reproduction or distribution of this copyrighted work is illegal. Criminal copyright infringement, including infringement without monetary gain, is investigated by the FBI and is punishable by up to 5 years in federal prison and a fine of $250,000.

Chapter One

Aspen Andrews stared blankly at the computer screen lost in her memories. There'd been so many times when she'd wondered if she'd ever find anything to replace the dream job she'd lost eighteen months earlier. And this was one of those moments. It had been a long, tough road, but for the most part, she was finally settling into her new gig. The bullet she'd taken in St. Maarten not only splintered ribs causing several puncture wounds in her lungs and various other *essential* organs, but it also sent her entire life careening in a different direction.

She'd been lucky, the woman she'd been protecting was one of the premier pediatric surgeons in the world. And, Dr. Cecelia Barnes hadn't hesitated to put those skills to work when Aspen leapt in front of the bullet meant for her. Even the small island's less than top-tier clinic hadn't dimmed the skilled doctor's ability to pull off one of her most miraculous saves. The brilliant brunette beauty had assured Aspen the pediatric label was misleading…all the parts were the same, the only difference had been the large *obstacles* on her chest. Evidently, pediatric patients rarely had 38D breasts.

CeCe Barnes had saved Aspen's life, but she hadn't been able to save her career as an Air Force pilot. The Air Force doctors had been impressed with Dr. Barnes' work, but their respect for her medical skills hadn't influenced their decision. They'd still stamped *Diminished Respiratory Capacity* at the top of their report. Those three words had ended Aspen's Air Force career.

It was truly astonishing how devastating a little ink, and a rubber stamp could be. She'd found it oddly anticlimactic to be sidelined by a single rifle shot after dodging surface to air missiles as a fighter pilot for several years. She'd discovered all to quickly the burning loyalty she'd felt toward the Air Force had been one sided.

The one bright point in the whole debacle was hearing from her friends how effectively CeCe had put Aspen's commanding officer in his place. When he'd shown up in her clinic on St. Maarten, Lt. Colonel Brian Riggs had tried to intimidate her with his formidable presence. Smiling to herself, Aspen still wished someone had videotaped it. She'd have loved to see the diminutive doctor set Riggs back on his heels. *All those cell phones in the room and not one of those yoyos thought to record the encounter? So much for all that nonsense about a YouTube generation.*

Kent West had roared with laughter when he recounted it later. "Damn, Asp, it was the funniest thing ever. The room was wall to fucking wall with former military men all standing a little straighter when those stripes stalked in the door. But Riggs's rank didn't mean a thing to Cecelia. It was great, the most powerful person in the room was an exhausted woman who didn't give two shits who...and I quote, 'Lieutenant Colonel Whoever' thought he was."

Aspen had finally threatened to ban Kent from her room if he didn't stop making her laugh—damn, laughing had been seriously painful those first few days. She'd been friends with the West boys and Jax McDonald since they were kids, and she couldn't remember ever seeing Kent laugh as hard as he had when he told her that particular story.

By the time she'd come out of surgery, all three of her childhood pals had been front and center. Their support hadn't surprised her, but it had been damned comforting. Kyle West's face had been the first thing she saw when she opened her eyes. The lines of worry erased in an instant when he smiled down at her. "Damn, baby-girl, you scared the shit out of us." From anyone else, the words would have sounded gruff, but from Kyle, they resounded with love.

When they'd been younger, her three best friends had been the only ones who'd understood her need for speed, and they'd enjoyed indulging her at every opportunity. Holy hell, it was no small miracle she hadn't gotten them all killed with her uncensored adventurous spirit before finally enlisting. The Air Force had shown her how to focus all that restless energy so it worked for her rather than sending her in a hundred different directions all at once. The three men had managed to track her while she'd been in the Air Force despite Jax's commitments in the NFL and the West brothers' own deployments. Kent and Kyle had made no secret of the fact she was under their protection...something she'd both appreciated and detested.

The only reason Uncle Sam hadn't cut Aspen loose after the St. Maarten clusterfuck was because her friends had gone to bat for her. And obviously saving Cecelia Barnes' life had also been a pretty big factor. It seemed helping out the wife of legendary former black ops agent, Cameron Barnes, was cause for special consideration. Cam was still extremely well-regarded in the upper echelons of the Pentagon, and his favor bought you a lot of latitude despite the fact the mission had been strictly off the books. Personally, she thought the words *former and retired* were questionable at best when referring to Cameron Barnes, but she had yet to prove he was still actively engaged in any mission work.

Aspen had been offered a position in the Department of Homeland Security that hadn't appealed to the adrenaline junkie in her. But, with no other viable options available, she'd accepted before she'd even been cleared to return to work. Her trust fund was locked up until she turned thirty and she'd promised herself she would avoid using any of the allowance she'd received. She'd always turned the stipends down, and preferred to make her way like everyone else.

After enduring eight grueling weeks of physical therapy at the hands of a tyrant calling himself a *restorative specialist*, Aspen had finally been cut loose. Her new employer hired a moving company to pack up her meager belongings, deposited them in a storage facility, and then promptly sent her to various scenic locales in B.F.E. Her boss hadn't been kidding when he'd used the acronym. Bum-fuck Egypt, indeed.

Robert Crane had to be a direct descendant of the fictional Ichabod Crane from the old animated movie. He was frightening brilliant, with instincts no one dared question, but he had the personality of a slice of unbuttered toast. And, listening to him speak was as good as any tranquilizer Aspen had ever taken. She'd nodded off in meetings so many times he'd sent her back to Walter Reed Hospital for a sleep study. Aspen was fairly certain his *recommendation* for the study had been more about punishment than a serious concern for her health, *the asshat*.

After losing her parents when she was thirteen, Aspen had drifted between the homes of several less than enthused relatives. The women were either jealous of the attention their significant others paid her, or hopeful she'd keep the men preoccupied so they could pursue their own extra-curricular activities. The fact her grandfather had the foresight to limit the use of her trust fund, hadn't helped to endear her to those tasked with helping her either.

Aspen's maternal grandfather hadn't approved of his only daughter's gypsy lifestyle or her marriage to an American without any visible means of supporting her. The old man hadn't been anyone's fool that was for sure. Hell, even Aspen realized how foolishly her parents spent money. They would have squandered anything her grandfather had given them.

You didn't amass a billion-dollar empire in the eastern bloc without being good at reading people, and from what she'd learned about him, her grandfather had possessed an uncanny ability to predict people's behavior. Knowing what people were going to do, gave him a huge advantage in business that he'd capitalized on. She'd been the only person he'd never fully understood. He might not have understood his adrenaline junkie granddaughter, but he'd certainly provided for her future.

Assigned to DHS's Office of Cyber Security meant she could work from almost anywhere in the U.S. Her superiors hadn't hesitated to send her bouncing around the country like a damned rubber ball. One of her first assignments had been to confirm the clearance on a man Uncle Sam wanted to recruit. The independent developer would be contracted to develop various software applications. It hadn't taken her long to discover Phoenix Morgan was exactly who he seemed to be. The fact he was the younger brother of a recently retired Navy SEAL might have gotten Phoenix's foot in the door, but it wasn't going to get him the contract without a full clearance.

During the sixty days she'd been given to *observe and investigate* Phoenix Morgan, Aspen had discovered a previously unrealized talent for on-line gaming. After she'd stopped to think about it...it actually made perfect sense. The thousands of hours she'd spent flying in virtual reality had programmed her brain for the type of role play required in the games she favored. Her supervisor hadn't sent her to Montana to personally observe the man, preferring she simply observe his on-line behavior. At first, she'd been relieved to stay put for a change, but after getting to know him, she'd regretted the distance.

Phoenix Morgan was a genius at developing games spanning a wide spectrum of ability and skill development—the reason the U.S. military wanted him on-board was a no-brainer. What was more difficult to understand was what the National Security Administration had in mind for him? For some reason, the man had fallen on the short list of people the NSA and DHS wanted for a "special project" but no one *in-the-know* was willing to talk.

One of Aspen's biggest downfalls in the military had been her curiosity. The Air Force's *need-to-know* mentality had driven her to distraction. If she was flying a mission intended to clear targets, she damned well felt like she *needed-to-know*, but the U.S. military rarely agreed. There had been a lot she loved about being a fighter pilot—but the aristocracy of information sharing hadn't been one of them.

Redirecting her attention to the laptop in front of her, Aspen smiled when she saw two different icons flashing on the screen. "Well, guys, it's about time. I was about to give up on you showing up tonight. Just because I mistakenly believed you were one and the same in the beginning doesn't mean I'm not on to your wily ways now. Since I happen to know you are on different continents tonight, you've just confirmed how close you are communicating in this little tag-team game of seduction you're playing."

Lacing her fingers together before rotating her wrists and flexing her fingers, Aspen couldn't hold back the grin spreading heat as it slid over her face. Damn, if she didn't look forward to the times, the three of them could play together.

She'd spent the day backtracking the asshat who had taken a sudden interest in Phoenix Morgan. And, just like the previous couple of weeks, the prick had managed to stay at least a step or two ahead of her. She was getting damned tired of playing fucking tag when she always seemed to be *it*. But his stalker was getting braver, so she didn't plan to back-off, Phoenix didn't know it yet, but he'd acquired a guardian angel.

Aspen had been working for twelve hours straight and really should have gotten some much needed sleep before hitting the road, but now that she'd seen Phoenix and Mitch were ready to play, sleep could wait. It was time to let off some steam. There was only so much she could do to protect him without actually meeting Phoenix. Even though that pleasure was on the agenda, but it wasn't going to happen tonight so gaming would have to do.

Her application to Mountain Mastery had been submitted. She hoped to meet him during one of his regular weekend visits to the BDSM club outside Billings that had recently become a hotspot among the Midwest's wealthy kinksters. With personal references from Kent, Kyle, and Jax, she wasn't worried about being accepted, but she wasn't naïve either. The owners of the club, the Ledek brothers would call the Prairie Winds Club to verify her information when they saw she'd also listed the three men as her emergency contacts.

The Mountain Mastery application had included all the usual elements...health information and restrictions, play experience, previous experience in the lifestyle in and out of club settings along with ample space to list both hard and soft limits. But it had also included something she hadn't been expecting—a request to write a fantasy scenario. Anticipating the leash her friends would demand Nate and Taz Ledek tie to her, Aspen had written a fantasy scenario she knew none of them would ever allow.

It was amazing how over the top her imagination could be when it was playing with a safety net. The hair on the back of her neck stood up, when she thought back on the moment, she'd hit the button sending the document to Nate's inbox. Trying to shake off the skittishness she felt, Aspen scrubbed her hands up and down her arms. Making an effort to push the feeling of foreboding aside, she refocused on the game in front of her. "Okay, guys, let's see how quickly I can mop the floor with you so I can get some sleep. Lots of miles to cover tomorrow, you know. Good guys to look out for and bad guys to track...I'm a busy girl, so let's get started."

Chapter Two

One week later

PHOENIX SHIFTED UNCOMFORTABLY in his padded office chair trying to relieve the unrelenting pressure of the zipper of his jeans branding his cock. At this point, he was probably going to have a permanent impression running the length of his unruly appendage. He'd spent the majority of the past year in a state of unsatisfied need with a perpetual hard-on. *I swear the damned woman is going to be the reason I start wearing sweats.*

Mitch's soft laughter had Phoenix turning around to see his friend leaning against the doorframe, sipping from a steaming cup of coffee. "Reading the fantasy portion of her application?"

"Yeah. Fuck. I'm telling you, the woman missed her calling, she should be writing kinky romance novels."

"I'm assuming you're thinking about how much her potential readers would benefit since we now know she doesn't need the money." And wasn't that the damned truth? Once they'd traced her laptop back to DHS, it hadn't taken long for Micah Drake at Prairie Winds to discover who they were dealing with. Oh yeah, the phone call he'd gotten from Jax McDonald had been tons of fun. *Not!* Of course, compared the similar call he'd gotten from Kent and Kyle West, his chat with Jax hadn't seemed so bad.

None of them had minced any words when they let him know Aspen Andrews was under their protection. As Doms, both Mitch and Phoenix understood exactly what their declarations meant, and they intended to honor their claim. But it didn't mean he wasn't planning to turn her lovely ass a nice shade of scarlet at his first opportunity. Damn, she'd been taunting both of them far too long to let her off scot free. *The little minx needs to pay the piper.*

"I think she wrote this thinking there was no way it could ever *actually* happen. There would be a certain freedom in writing from the heart when you didn't anticipate ever actually having to reenact the scene." Phoenix had been playing strategy games with *Athena* for over a year, and he'd spent the past few months meticulously studying every move as he critically analyzed each word. The woman had chosen her name well, she was definitely a goddess of war strategy.

"I agree, but I also think it was written from the depths of her soul. You heard what Kyle said, she negotiated a five-year membership to the Prairie Winds Club when they pulled her off leave to help protect CeCe. She didn't care jack-squat about the money, but the membership assured her that her friends would have her back and accept her foray into the lifestyle." Hell, she'd been fucking fearless on that mission. Never batting an eye at anything they set in front of her. "For a woman who was used to the emotional distance of being a fighter pilot, she'd hit the ground running from the moment she joined the team. She didn't let up until that fucking *capo* Craig Allen's bullet dropped her like a sack of sugar."

During the time they'd been friends, Phoenix had noticed Mitch's Cajun childhood accent surfaced when he was upset or angry. So, his reference to Cecelia Barnes' stalker as a *capo* or coward, told him the man was more affected by the conversation than he appeared. His facial expression had remained impassive, but his eyes were spitting fire. Phoenix leaned back against the plush black leather and crossed his arms over his chest. Giving Mitch a considering look, he asked, "I've only gotten bits and pieces of this story, care to fill in the blanks?"

There wasn't any question in Phoenix's mind that Mitch Ames would prefer to erase the memory of that day, but he was equally sure the information was important. Anything in Mitch and Aspen's shared past that had the power to elicit such a strong response needed to be out in the open. As a Dom, Phoenix knew it was his responsibility to uncover anything that might be an emotional trigger for the submissive in his care, and this had all the hallmarks of a hell of a minefield.

MITCH UNDERSTOOD PHOENIX'S need to know all the details of what had taken place in St. Maarten because there was little doubt it had shaped who Aspen Andrew's was today. Hell, it led directly to the creation of her on-line persona as Athena.

He had always regretted the fact he hadn't been able to stay in St. Maarten long enough to explore their mutual attraction. But, that didn't mean he hadn't carefully tracked her recovery. She'd made remarkable progress, but some of the damage had been irreversible. Everybody but Aspen had known her career as a fighter pilot was over as soon as Craig Allen's bullet pierced her side. Scrubbing his hand over his face, Mitch tried, once again, unsuccessfully to purge the picture from his memory.

Seeing Aspen lying lifeless on the ground, knowing his own shot, the one ending the threat to Cecelia, had come a split second too late, continued to haunt him. It didn't matter how many times he reviewed the tape or how many people applauded what was always referred to as *the shot of a lifetime*. All he saw was Aspen's body jerk to the side from the impact before she crumpled to the ground. Pushing away from the doorframe in hopes changing his physical position would push the picture from his mind, Mitch settled in one of the other office chairs and leaned back.

"Long story short, Aspen was tapped to help protect Dr. Cecelia Barnes. Micah Drake at Prairie Winds, doing what he does best, knew Aspen was on leave in New York City which put her exactly where we needed her. She helped gather intel and was the first to spot our target before flying to St. Maarten. Once there, she made sure their paths crossed at the airport. Hell, she even snowed him into thinking he'd picked her up. After agreeing to spend a few days with him on his yacht, she slipped him a mickey and searched the yacht—the woman was fucking fearless." It had been her greatest advantage and her downfall.

"Allen hadn't been aiming at Aspen, he'd taken a bead on Dr. Barnes. His shot would have gone straight through Cecelia's heart. Aspen saw him and knew instinctively what was going to happen. She didn't even hesitate before putting herself between the bullet and the woman she was supposed to be protecting."

"I can't imagine St. Maarten having the best medical facilities for that sort of injury." Hell, Phoenix doubted there was more than a handful of islands in the region with well-equipped trauma units.

"Ordinarily you'd have been right. But Cecelia's husband had recently started rebuilding the local clinic into a state of the art facility in the hope he could convince her to move her practice to the island. Not all of the equipment had been updated, and the truth is, it Cecelia Barnes' iron will and skill that saved Aspen's life.

The clinic she owns in Houston still draws patients from all over, but then it's well known that she's one of the best pediatric surgeons in the world. Her innovative techniques have changed the face of surgery not only for her young patients, but her methods have impacted procedures for adults as well."

There wasn't a doctor in the entire world Mitch respected more than Cecelia Barnes. The miracle she'd pulled off that day was just one in a long line of incredible medical feats on her resume. Shaking his head, Mitch couldn't hold back his laughter. "CeCe insists Cam, her husband, and Dom is the real hero because he had all the tools in place. But, those tools would have been completely useless in anyone else's hands."

"Tell me about her injury." The bits and pieces Phoenix picked up from the reports he'd read hadn't detailed much beyond the fact her survival had been nothing short of a miracle.

"The bullet caused slivering of a couple of ribs. Those slivers making one projectile fracture and become thirty. The bone chards sliced, diced, and punctured everything in their path. If CeCe hadn't been on her game, Aspen wouldn't have even made it to the clinic." Every person associated with the mission had been damned impressed watching her transformation from the terrified target into the take charge physician. Mitch had seen battle hardened medics fold under less pressure.

"Unfortunately, the damage to her lungs was significant enough for Uncle Sam to end her career as a pilot. It would have been little more than a blip on the radar for a civilian pilot." Every man there had gone to the wall for her, but in the end, Captain Aspen Andrews lost the job she loved.

"So how did she end up working for DHS?" Mitch assumed Phoenix new more than he was letting on, but he understood his friend's need for confirmation. They'd been tracking Athena for longer than either of them had anticipated it would take, and now that they had her in their sights, neither of them wanted to make a misstep and send her scampering out of reach again.

"Cameron Barnes never fully retired—despite appearances to the contrary. The truth is, he was so deep for so long I doubt Uncle Sam will ever completely let him go—at least not until he is too old to be of any use. He doesn't take many missions, but he is the intelligence officer and strategic specialist far more often than anyone realizes. The man is a relentless enemy, but he's a damn loyal friend. Saving his beloved wife's life wasn't an act he looked upon lightly. CeCe isn't just Cam's wife and submissive—she's his entire world. He readily admits she and their daughter are his reason for existing."

"So Cameron Barnes was responsible for Aspen landing the DHS job, but how did she end up as Athena?"

Mitch laughed. "You already know you were her first assignment. What better way to get inside your head than to play against you? Personally, I think she enjoyed the games so much she continued even after she'd filed her report."

"From what I've been able to learn, she originally thought I was playing as myself and as Cajun Warrior."

Mitch had the same impression, he'd used the name as a shield to prevent anyone from linking him to the character he played in the games. Anyone trying to fly under the radar as a black ops operative didn't need to give the bad guys any additional information about how their mind worked. The real question was why she'd kept playing after she'd figured out he and Phoenix were two different people?

"That is an interesting twist, isn't it? But I think she's discovered an outlet for the part of her who will always be Captain Andrews, Air Force pilot. Soldiers may retire, but a part of their soul is always poised and ready just at the fringe of battle-ready mode. Of course, this explains her affinity for the piloting portion of your games." Mitch knew he'd practically growled the last sentence, but damn, the woman had mopped the floor with both of them more times than he could remember.

"Okay, so I feel like I have a better grasp on what makes her tick, but that doesn't mean I understand this." He waved the sheaf of papers he still held in his hand. After his conference call with Nate and Taz last night, they'd reluctantly sent him a copy of the portions of her application a Dom interested in a particular submissive would have access to.

Everything had been fairly standard until he'd gotten to the fantasy portion. Mitch wasn't thrilled with how little she'd listed on her limit list, but he chalked it up to inexperience. But her narrative writing describing her fantasy had blown his mind. He'd been driving to the ranch and used a text to speech app so he could listen to the short story while driving, but it hadn't taken long for him to see some of the language was beyond the sweet voice of the program. It hadn't actually mattered because he'd heard enough to make him almost drive off the road more than once. Hell, he'd listened to it twice before he'd forwarded the document to Phoenix.

Nate had incorporated the free-write section in the club's application hoping it would serve as a window into the mind of the sub. From what Mitch understood, his *experiment* was turning out to be a valuable tool. If Aspen's biography and fantasy were anything to go by, he could certainly understand how useful the short essays could be. Damn, the thing was a window directly into her soul. It was loaded with information, a lot of which Mitch doubted she'd intended to share. Underneath the soldier turned agent, was a little girl who's only real experience with love and acceptance had been with the three young men who'd taken her under their wing when she was still in grade school.

The night Aspen was shot in St. Maarten, Kent West found Mitch standing outside the clinic's back door. He hadn't prayed in more years than he could remember, but that night had been the exception. He'd been so relieved to learn she'd pulled through surgery he'd slipped outside to send up a prayer of thanks to a God he wasn't sure even remembered his name. Kent slid into the shadows with him and added his own prayer of thanks for the woman he'd called a friend since they'd been kids.

Kent's voice had drifted over the warm, moist night air, "I'll never forget the first time I saw Aspen. She was wearing a pink dress with what looked like an apron, our mom told us later it was called a pinafore—whatever the hell that is. Anyway, she was standing against the fence watching the other kids play. She was so damned skinny and despite her fancy dress and shiny patent leather shoes it was easy to see nobody really cared about being her friend—the lost look in her eyes made me sad."

Mitch heard the melancholy in Kent's voice and wondered how bad it had been for the former Navy SEAL to still feel so strongly about something that had happened more than two decades earlier. "I got Kyle and Jax, and the three of us went over to talk to her. We weren't too much older, but we were already a lot bigger than she was. I can still remember the terrified look on her face as we walked toward her. Years later, she told us she almost peed her pants she'd been so scared when she realized we were walking toward her." Kent's soft chuckle eased some of Mitch's tension, and the rest of his story had been a lesson in a level of compassion rare among young kids.

"From that day forward, everybody in the school knew she was our friend. They treated her with respect, or they answered to us. When she figured out we'd be changing schools a year ahead of her, she studied hard enough to be advanced a grade. Her military records confirm what the three of us already knew, the woman is a fucking genius. Uncle Sam screwed up when he didn't send her directly into military intelligence, she's a natural military analyst. She can identify strategic and tactical strengths and weaknesses at a glance. The amazing part is it appears to be an innate skill—but all that aside, she'd have been miserable stuck in some underground think tank."

Mitch shook his head at the memory, recounting the experience made him feel like a fool for not putting two and two together. Looking at Phoenix, Mitch shrugged. "Anyway, in hindsight, I probably should have zeroed in on Aspen as Athena—and I know Kent is kicking himself for not thinking of her. Hell, you and I didn't make any attempt to keep our search a secret, yet none of us put it together. Not exactly our best work." Mitch couldn't hold back his chuckle at the irony. Their team was renowned for their instincts and ability to piece together seemingly disconnected fragments of information, but they'd all missed this one.

"Sometimes it's hard to see an answer when the evidence drifts in slowly. I'm just grateful we finally know who we're dealing with, and I'm relieved we haven't been chasing some fifty-year-old unemployed guy living in his mother's basement." Phoenix shuddered, making the papers he was holding rattle. When Mitch chuckled at his revulsion, Phoenix shook his head. "I'm serious man, you have no idea how many times *that* particular scenario played out in my mind. Fucking terrifying." Mitch wasn't going to admit how many times he'd worried about the same thing.

"Understood. But now we need to focus on what we're going to do about Athena's fantasy. According to my sources, she's on her way to Montana as we speak." Mitch paused, because there was one particular element in Aspen's fantasy that continued to come to the forefront each time he read it. "There are a hundred points I believe have come from the deepest parts of her soul, but there is one I find myself coming back to time and time again."

"Two masters?" Mitch nodded at Phoenix's inquiry. "I agree; the entire story is a walk through her deepest desires. It's a psychoanalyst's dream come true." Mitch watched Phoenix attempt to smooth the edges of the papers he'd crinkled while reading her fantasy. "And she obviously plans on spending some time at Mountain Mastery or she wouldn't have applied for membership. We need to talk to Nate as soon as possible." Phoenix already had a plan in mind, he was just waiting to see if Mitch was thinking along the same lines. "I think she deserves a proper Montana welcome. The sky isn't the only thing big here, we're known for being very *accommodating* as well."

This time, Mitch laughed out loud. "Well now, if that's the case, let's see what we can do about making sure Aspen aka Athena understands just how committed we are to making sure her dreams come true."

Chapter Three

My Fantasy

AFTER MY PARENTS had died, I was forced to grow up too fast. I had to move away from my three best friends. They'd been my sole support system for years, and the only way I knew to cope was to create a fantasy world in my mind. In my imagination, I became a fearless warrior who battled evil wherever I found it. And most important, my new alter ego didn't have to worry about being taken advantage of when she found herself at home with one of the male relatives who'd been charged with Aspen's care.

When the men of the house figured out they'd only be getting a small stipend, without the unlimited access to my trust fund they'd expected, they quickly decided there were other ways for me to pay for their hospitality. I didn't dare tell my friends…I knew full well what they'd do, and I didn't want their futures jeopardized coming to my defense.

My warrior-self became a champion of other victims. She protected them, she nurtured them, and in the process, she learned to read the enemy with an almost other-worldly accuracy. But there was always a part of her wishing for two special men who would take her…protect her as she'd done for so many others. They'd earn the submission they had originally demanded, and the great Athena would give it willingly in the end.

During a fierce battle, she'd be captured and become a spoil of war. The common soldiers would cast lots for the right to claim the great Athena. The Greek goddess of war strategy would finally be powerless over her own fate. What follows is Athena's personal account of her capture and how her captors became her saviors.

I'VE RUN OUT of places to hide. The enemy has me cornered in one of the smaller areas of the palace. The servants call this space the war room because it's where I meet with military leaders. It isn't overly large, but it's never needed to be. I've always had a clear vision of where the battles would take place and how they would play out, making it easy to direct my army. But this time, I've misjudged things and underestimated my enemies. I know it's only a matter of time before they storm through the doors and lead me out of my home in chains. One small miscalculation was all it took…my demise far too easy for those who now yearn to make an example of me.

Despite the warm weather, I don layers of clothing hoping the soldiers who pull me from the palace won't rip all the garments from me. I don't want to be paraded through the streets naked. Humiliation will be more punishment than I can bear…I experienced too much of it as a child. I'm not afraid of pain, but humiliation is beyond my endurance. The servants are hiding in the lower levels of the palace where they are safe. But, I know the soldiers will have no interest in them. I am their prize.

The palace is grand, fit for a goddess, but it isn't filled with things. I've always preferred sharing wealth rather than accumulating objects. There will be little for the soldiers to steal and that will only serve to further enrage them. Now that I consider their reaction, I wish I'd added another layer of clothing as they're sure to be angrier than I'd originally assumed.

I hear the shouts of triumph as soon as they burst through the front door directly below where I'm hiding. Their voices become *louder as they come thundering up the stairs. It won't be long now, my freedom is fleeting, it feels much like the final grains of sand draining from the hourglass. When the door splinters, the first thing I notice is the stench. The men who grasp my upper arms are drenched in sweat and reek of days spent fighting without the benefit of bathing. I fight the urge to gag, the stench makes my stomach roll.*

My mind shuts down; their taunts fall on deaf ears. I'm not listening as they pummel me with questions, nor am I concerned when they shred the top layers of clothing I'm using as a soldier would a shield. I'm blindfolded before being pulled toward the stairs, but my feet can't gain purchase, and I stumble, which angers them even more.

The irony of being yelled at for stumbling over stone steps I cannot see isn't lost on me. Their grip on my arms tightens, even more, becoming so painful I realize I'm becoming dizzy from holding my breath. I know they are marking me in ways I'll feel and see in the days to come, but my body and mind are functioning on different levels allowing me to finally find the strength to push aside the pain.

Before they cross the threshold of the front door, a sharp voice from behind us halts their progress. No one moves for long seconds, and then I feel it...the unmistakable movement of air so close I can feel the difference in energy. "You're marking what is ours. You were told not to hurt her." The men holding me react immediately to the newcomer's growled words by loosening their grip and I nearly sag to the floor. By some miracle, my knees don't fold, and I'm glad because I suddenly realize my hands have gone numb from their brutal grip, and I wouldn't have had any defense against the fall.

I am unsteady on my feet, weaving precariously from side-to-side. Before I can reach out to steady myself, strong arms wrap around me from behind, pulling me against a rock-hard chest. But there is no malice in this man's touch, just a quiet strength holding me upright. Warm breath brushes over the side of my neck making me shiver despite the fact I'm sweltering beneath all the clothing. "A goddess indeed. Stunning despite the armor she wears." Another man's soft laughter is so close in front of me I fear taking a deep breath because I'm sure my breasts will brush against him simply by raising from the inhalation.

"Using the extra layers to prevent being dragged naked through the streets, Athena?"

"Yes." There is no reason to lie, I know my body will give me away if I try. Something deep inside me is responding to these men, but I don't understand why. I feel lost, adrift, and it's unnerving.

"You didn't try to lie to us, I am pleased. Your honesty will be rewarded later. First, we need to strip off these extra layers, we won't allow you to hide beneath them. And you're far too hot, love." His rich voice resonates to the depths of my soul igniting feelings I'm struggling to understand. They are unfamiliar, and I'm not yet comfortable feeling my body respond in such ways. Reminding myself the men surrounding me aren't interested in what is best for me is difficult when my blood is pooling between my legs making my entire body throb with need.

They waste no time stripping me down to the soft peplos covering my linen undergarments. Their hands stilling when there was little between their touch and my bare skin. I know they plan to claim my body just as they will claim victory in this battle, but I also know losing one battle does not mean I've lost the war.

It's difficult for me to concentrate as everything around me begins to shift and the historical elements that surround me begin to recede. In seconds, the past has faded, and I'm standing in the middle of a small stage, a soft spotlight shining down making the white linen shift I'm wearing all but disappear. I'm no longer blindfolded, but the light makes it impossible for me to see clearly beyond a couple of feet in front of me.

I'm reeling from how quickly things have changed, my mind

spins as I try to clear the questions bouncing around in my head. I'd been fighting to wrap my mind around the way my body responded to the men who'd snatched me from the clutches of the soldiers. Now I'm fighting a new battle...one I don't stand a chance to win when I can barely stand on my own. I feel myself beginning to sway as my mind spins in circles, but warm hands still me before I can fall. "I've got you, love. Hold still while we secure you. We'll get your punishment out of the way first and then we'll see to the pleasure your body craves."

A cool band of silk slides over my eyes once again and I find my mind beginning to float into a place where nothing exists but the soft brush of warm hands at my wrists and ankles. The place my mind escapes to is safe and secure but detached from the reality of my situation. The sound of fabric being shredded startles me back to the moment, and I realize the garment I'd been wearing is now gone. "Beautifully bare, I do love a smooth pussy. We'll make sure you keep those spa appointments, baby." *This voice is familiar...I've heard it before in another time and place. I remember being lost in its timbre once before while I walked through the fog. I'd tried to find a way to him then, but the fog was too thick and I'd slipped too far away before he was gone.*

This time, I find my voice and whisper, "Don't go. Please don't leave me again." *I remember feeling so alone the last time he left even though I still can't remember where we met. I don't think I can bear him leaving me again.*

"I'm not going anywhere, cher." *I'm close to bringing the memory into focus when the first stinging blow lands on my ass causing me to gasp in surprise. As I shudder through the strikes, my mind once again drifts to another plane. The pain morphs into a whole new kind of heat, searing through my blood, igniting a firestorm of need that quickly sends a wash of moisture to my sex. The first trickles of evidence snake down the insides of my thighs as the final swat rocks me as far up onto my toes as the straps binding me allow.*

Hot fingers slide through my drenched folds and for the first time I'm grateful for the shield the blindfold affords. The absurdity of my ostrich theory isn't lost on me, but in the absence of any other way to hide how deeply affected I was by their punishment, I'll cling to any small piece of dignity I can.

"Don't try to hide your reaction, Athena. It won't work and will just piss us off. Your body craves what we can give you. Knowing how deeply your submissive streak runs pleases me more than I can say." His fingers curl inside me, touching the spot I know will immediately launch me into the abyss of orgasm, and it does.

Colors flash around me like a kaleidoscope of neon lightning as pleasure races through my body with such intensity I'm only cognizant for a few seconds...a few precious seconds so intense I feel myself burning from the inside out even as I'm sliding into a sweet respite. Instinctively, I know once I reach the new level of consciousness I'll be able to float in a quiet space and gather the shattered pieces of my mind back together before I'm forced to face the men who now own me body and soul.

Chapter Four

MITCH READ THE fantasy portion of Aspen's application so many times he was starting to feel like a damned stalker. The entire thing was loaded with crystal clear glimpses into her subconscious. He doubted she'd taken the time to reread it before sending it off or she'd have known how telling it was. "There's a lot there. I'd be surprised if she intended to share such personal insights. I just can't see the woman I met in St. Maarten taking this circuitous route. Even now, during our on-line conversations, she's been direct almost to a fault."

"Not about her location or identity," Phoenix's tone reminded Mitch of a kid who'd been beaten at his own game, and it was actually pretty close to the truth in this particular case.

"Stop and think for a minute. She told us from the beginning she didn't intend to share that information and she stayed true to her word despite our continued badgering. If you'll think back, she gave us a couple of clues, but we failed to realize it at the time." And she had. She'd told them she was a tumbling tumbleweed, and according to their DHS sources, Aspen had been assigned to several locations during her short tenure with the agency.

"Whatever. I'm still going to take out my frustration on her lovely ass. And from the pictures I've seen, my hand is going to fit nicely across those nice rounded cheeks. She's going over my lap the first chance I get." Mitch wanted to laugh out loud at his friend's justification for getting Athena exactly where she'd have been anyway.

Phoenix obviously wasn't accustomed to being beaten at much of anything—and particularly not his own games. When Mitch rolled in late last night, he'd followed Kip's truck into the yard. The youngest Morgan brother had greeted him with his typical boisterous bull shit, but he'd also told Mitch how glad he was they'd finally managed to track down Athena.

"Damn, Phoenix has been a real pain in the ass for months. I'm glad Miss Andrews will now be on the receiving end of my brother's pissy attitude; I'm done with it. Fucking hell, I'm telling you my brothers are four for four. Every one of them has gone completely bat shit crazy until they got the girl." They'd each grabbed a beer and settled on the back deck watching the stars move slowly across the Montana sky. "You know one of the strangest things about it is that every single one of my older brothers preached my entire life about how there is always a girl to replace the one you lose."

"That's probably not the way it works when it's the right woman." Mitch rocked his chair back on two legs and propped his boots up on the adjacent seat giving him an amazing view of the stars above. He loved gazing at the night sky, it was easy to understand why Montana was known as the Big Sky state. The vastness of space was easier to imagine when it was spread out in front of you. It was humbling to know just how small our little corner, we call home, of the universe really is.

"I keep telling Phoenix he'd feel better if he'd go down to Mountain Mastery and blow off some steam, but he hasn't been there to play for months." Kip shook his head, and Mitch would have laughed at his obvious frustration, but there was a part of him that actually understood Kip's point. And the hell of it was, a big part of him missed being Kip's age and believing there wasn't much that couldn't be solved with a good drunk or fucking a beautiful woman until you were both too spent to walk.

"I don't know how much he's told you, but we've learned a lot about Ms. Andrews in the last few days—that's one of the reasons I'm rolling in so late. Hang on to your hat, because Phoenix and I are definitely going to be playing at the club in the near future." There wasn't a chance in hell they'd walk away from the challenge Aspen's Mountain Mastery application presented.

Kip's raised brow let Mitch know his curiosity had been piqued, but he wasn't going to ask any questions—at least not yet. "I'm pooped, and I've got a shit-ton of stuff to get done before the A.I. team shows up Monday." Phoenix had mentioned Kip was making some changes to the Morgan's ranching operation. Evidently those changes would include artificial insemination. Certainly didn't sound like anything Mitch wanted to be involved in. Kip started shaking his head and laughing. "Damn, man. It's not like anybody is asking you to be on probe duty or anything, so you can wipe the horrified look off your face. Although, watching a couple of our best bulls give it up to a little electrical stimulation will make you mighty glad you're at the top of the food chain."

"I'll take your word for it. I'm convinced this is one of those *ignorance is bliss* things." Mitch knew far more about the process than he was letting on, but awareness and a desire to witness it firsthand were two entirely different things. "Besides, I've come to plot Athena's demise with your brother, and I'd hate to leave it all to him. I fear he might go too far and push her so far away we won't ever be able to reel her in, and I think she just might be what we've been looking for."

"Figured you guys might be planning to share a woman. Seems to be working out well for Brandt and Ryan, although I'm not sure what Joelle would tell you. Those two keep pretty close tabs on her." Mitch had heard the same thing, word tended to travel quickly among former Special Forces operatives. For the most part, they remained a tight knit group long after leaving the teams.

"From what I've seen, Joelle holds her own quite nicely. To tell you the truth, every polyamorous relationship I've seen works well, so I'm anxious to see where this leads. I'm sure there are a lot of reasons for the success of poly relationships, but the most obvious is because they require a lot of special attention. Kent West once told me he and Kyle had grown up seeing how dedicated their dads were to making sure their mom always felt cared for. They had great role models for the kind of life they wanted for themselves. I envy them, and I'm grateful for their openness."

"You have to admire brothers who can get along well enough to share a wife. None of us have similar enough tastes in women to share." Kip laughed, but Mitch suspected his words were only partially true. He'd seen all of the Morgans interacting with Coral, Joelle, and Josie. The brothers' love and respect for the women who'd joined their family was easy to see. It was also clear there were similar traits among the women, but he'd leave that discussion for another time.

PHOENIX'S TEASING TONE brought Mitch back to the moment. "Damn, I don't know where you went, but it was a damned long way from here because you haven't heard a word I've said." Mitch didn't even try to hold back his grin. Hell, he'd never met anybody who could become as lost in his work as Phoenix Morgan. *Hello pot, meet kettle.* He'd watched his friend zero in on a laptop so completely he hadn't even heard his own phone ringing on the table beside him. From what he'd heard, Sage had been the same way before his life was turned upside down by three beautiful, but very active little girls.

"I was just thinking about my conversation with Kip last night. We arrived at the same time and shared a beer outside." Phoenix looked up from the copy of Aspen's application he was holding, raising a brow in question. Mitch grinned. "That young man is going to go down fighting when the right woman comes into his life."

"That's the truth. Part of that is due to the fact he's the youngest of five boys and likely to have sustained more than a few *unintentional* head injuries. Another issue is our mother relentlessly pushing him to date the neighbor girl. Not that Caila isn't nice enough—but she is known as Calamity for a reason." Mitch didn't even try to hold back his laughter. No wonder Kip didn't seem too enthused about the idea of one woman in his life forever.

"Is the young lady still your neighbor?" Mitch was suddenly beginning to understand some of Kip's reluctance. Hell, no man wanted his mother to choose his wife.

"She's been away at school, but I heard she's coming back home to help her dad at his vet clinic. I saw her in town yesterday, and I can hardly wait for Kip to see her Monday." This time, it was Mitch's turn to look at his friend in question. "Oh, you're going to love this. Caila

Cooper is the A. I. *expert* her dad is bringing to oversee the semen collection from the ranch's bulls." His expression must have given away his revulsion because Phoenix burst out laughing. "Damn, buddy, tell me how you really feel about it."

"Fuck you. I was just wondering what on Earth your mother is thinking trying to match her son up with a woman who specializes in semen collection. You have to admit it sounds a bit odd." Particularly since he'd checked YouTube just before dawn. Jesus, Joseph, and sweet mother Mary, he couldn't imagine his own mother finding that particular skill set valuable in a potential daughter-in-law. But then again, he wasn't Kip Morgan either.

PHOENIX HAD TO remind himself that just because Mitch had divided his childhood between his parent's southern Louisiana mansion and their penthouse in Houston, it didn't mean he was a country boy. Hell, as near as he could tell, the only thing the man knew about livestock was which cut of steak he liked best. *I'd love to be able to see the picture he has in his mind of Calamity because there's no way in hell it's even close to the stunning young woman I saw walking down the street yesterday.* In fact, she'd reminded him a lot of the pictures he'd seen of Aspen Andrews.

For the first time in years, Phoenix was actually looking forward to helping with the bulls. He agreed with Kip, switching their emphasis to the sale of semen from their pure bred bulls had the potential to turn the entire ranching operation around. They had a reputation herd and had been selling bulls for years, but the new generation of ranchers' focus was different from the traditional cow-calf operations of the past. Kip's plan was solid and his turn around time to recoup the money they'd invested in equipment was impressive. The youngest Morgan brother seemed to be finally coming into his own, and Phoenix was happy to see things falling into place for him.

"I've set up a meeting with Nate for this afternoon. We've got to get everything finalized so he can get the word out to the club's membership."

"Do you foresee any challenges?" Phoenix understood Mitch's concern—in the more metropolitan clubs in large urban areas, last minute changes would meet with opposition, but here people were a lot more laid back. Phoenix wouldn't be opposed to living in other locations for short periods of time, but Montana would always be home.

"No. It isn't uncommon for there to be last minute changes. Nate sends out texts and emails so nobody is blindsided when something special is going down. Honestly, I think attendance will actually go up because there's nothing like a little role-playing to get the subs in the mood to play."

Mitch nodded. "Agreed. But I want to make sure anyone who plans to participate is properly cleared. We can't forget we're dealing with a DHS/NSA agent, she may be there on her own time, but as anybody who works for Uncle Sam knows—there really isn't any such thing as *your own time*."

"Brandt said the same thing. He and Ryan will be there with Joelle. Personally, I'd assumed it was one of those *once a SEAL, always a SEAL* things, but I can see your point. I'm guessing all you Special Forces guys have a pretty strong sense of protecting former fellow soldiers. I get the same vibe from Taz." And wasn't that the understatement of the year?

Phoenix knew Mitch had been a Ranger before moving into the Green Berets. Nate Ledek and his brother, Taz were both former Navy SEALs, and Taz was also a member of the Prairie Winds team. Kent and Kyle headed up a private covert ops team specializing in rescue missions, but they weren't averse to taking jobs for Uncle Sam when the circumstances were right. Phoenix respected the Wests' team and lent his support any time he could.

"Taz has a protective streak a mile wide when it comes to women in general, and if it's a woman he knows personally it's even worse. Be forewarned, he can be a real pain in the ass if he doesn't think the scene is going to play out in the submissive's favor." Phoenix wasn't surprised by Mitch's assessment because he'd seen the same trait in Nate. Both of the Ledek brothers were sexual Dominants, but their soft spot for women wasn't ever far below the surface.

"I'm not sure we can pull this thing together in six days. Hell, the costumes alone are going to be a challenge. I have no idea where to get a gown for a Greek Goddess."

"That's easy, we'll just do a Google search." Phoenix knew his expression had given away his skepticism when Mitch laughed. "Seriously, it's the soldier's clothing that will be a bigger problem—trust me, I've already started looking. And what I've come up with isn't anything I want to be seen in. Damn, why couldn't her fantasy be set in the old west?"

Phoenix laughed out loud at his friend's frustration, but agreed, the costumes weren't going to work for him either. "Well, I don't think the Doms clothing has to be period appropriate, but I'm going to lobby for the subs to all be dressed properly—or better yet improperly."

"And as obsessively detail oriented as I know you are—

Nate is worse, so I'm going to table my concern until after our phone conference. Now, I need something more than coffee to get me through the day, so either I'm going to have to brave the kitchen and risk dealing with your nieces or drive into Pine Creek." Phoenix winced when he looked at his watch drawing a chuckle from Mitch. "Town it is. Let's go."

Chapter Five

ASPEN REACHED FOR the ornate door handle just as the heavy wood door leading to Mountain Master swung away from her. She'd already been leaning forward in anticipation of the door's weight, so her forward momentum sent her nose first into a hard male chest. "Captain Andrews? Are you alright?" The voice was deep and reminded her of Taz Ledek, but there was an air of distance that told her it wasn't her friend's chest she'd fallen into.

For a second her brain short-circuited and before she could stop herself, she blurted out the first thing that went through her head. "Wow, you smell terrific." She felt her face heat with embarrassment. *Damn, I can't believe I said that out loud. Way to make a great impression...geez.* "Oh, yes, sorry. I wasn't...well, I wasn't expecting the door to open on its own."

"It didn't open on its own, sweetness. I opened it because I saw you drive through the gate." Damn, she'd forgotten about the electronic gate she'd driven through just a few minutes earlier. The man's sudden appearance had temporarily shut down her brain. No wonder he'd known she was coming. No doubt the hottie manning the gate and checking identification against the list on his clipboard had alerted his boss she'd arrived. Aspen had been so focused on getting through this interview she hadn't been alert and that was the last thing the club owner would want to see in a submissive applying for membership.

Oh yeah, she definitely recognized Nathanial Ledek. She'd done her homework, and with her security clearance, she'd been able to read more than his dull-as-dirt bio on the club's website. Most of his mission work was still classified, but there had been enough for her get a pretty solid idea about who he was as a person. Their on-line communication had been polite but oddly formal and now, standing in front of him it wasn't hard to see why.

There was a professional air of authority surrounding him. *And he's flipping huge.* When she'd asked Kent about Mountain Mastery's owner, he'd only told her one thing…that his nickname was *Big*. She'd been in the military long enough to know better than to ask how he'd gotten the tag, but now she wondered if the name was about his height rather than the size of his cock. *Damn, I really need to get laid. My brain is pickled in underutilized hormones and turning everything into something sexual.*

"I would sure like to know what you're thinking. Your breathing has become shallow and fast, your heartrate picked up, and your pupils have dilated until there is nothing but a narrow ring of color left. Very interesting indeed." Nathanial Ledek's voice held a hint of teasing, but she'd spent enough time with Doms to know there was an underlying command in his words as well.

She might know he expected an answer, but she wasn't going there. Technically she wasn't a member yet, and she was going to hang on to her secrets for as long as she could. Following him inside, she could have sworn she felt a shift in the energy when they entered his office. She stopped just inside the door trying to identify the strange feelings washing over her. The hair on the back of her neck stood up, and she'd learned a long time ago how foolish it was to ignore the precious sixth sense that had saved her ass on so many occasions.

"Captain Andrews?" She knew Nate had sensed the minute she stopped because he turned to face her.

Aspen didn't answer immediately, she let her eyes scan the room until they came to rest on the large mirror behind his ornately carved desk. There was a door near the corner of the room, she probably wouldn't have noticed it if she hadn't been looking. Any hope she'd held for confidentiality evaporated into mist and Aspen realized she was more disappointed than angry. She didn't say anything, just nodded to the mirror and turned on her heel to leave.

NATE COULDN'T BELIEVE it—damn, Aspen Andrews' instincts were fucking spot on. She'd sensed she was being watched the second she stepped into his office. He'd read her file and suspected those instincts had been fine-tuned during the years she'd spent bouncing between relatives who hadn't wanted her without access to her money. Damn, his friends better not let her go or Nate and every other Dom at the club would be fighting to claim her.

There was something about her—something wild simmering just below the surface, he knew would attract Doms like magnets to steel. Taz had warned him that she was nobody's fool, but Kyle had insisted she would be too distracted to tune in to the fact she was being observed. Both West brothers were watching via a sat-link, and he could hear them cursing under their breaths through the earbud he wore. *Yeah, you ass hats didn't listen to Taz, and now I'm the one in the hot seat.*

Why anyone would discount Taz's warning was a mystery to Nate. His brother had definitely inherited their Native American grandmother's *gift* of hearing from the heart. Nate was good at reading people, but he'd always known his ability was more about training than innate ability. He envied his brother's ability to know what someone was thinking or feeling, despite Taz's insistence, there were both good and bad elements attached to the gift.

Nate didn't intend to lie to her, but he damned well wasn't going to tell her everything either. "Stop." He wasn't surprised when she stopped dead in her tracks before doing a perfectly executed about turn. He bit back a smile—she hadn't been out of the Air Force long enough for those habits to have faded. As a former Navy SEAL, he'd cared more about staying alive than military protocol, but as a Dom, he understood the value of discipline. He recognized it in Aspen's movements, and respected it.

Studying her, Nate was amazed at the fire he saw— hell, her eyes were practically shooting sparks. "Yes?" The sharp tone of her voice broke through his thoughts. If she belonged to him, it would have earned her a paddling despite the fact he'd heard the underlying disappointment in the question. He and Taz would enjoy teaching her there were far more effective ways to express emotions than lashing out.

"I'm impressed, more than you know, with your instincts. And I want to encourage you to always trust them, particularly when your personal safety is on the line. But I'll also remind you that every aspect of this interview, down to the timing, has been done for your benefit. You are right, our conversation isn't going to be completely confidential, but neither is it going to be open to anyone who is a threat to you."

She didn't respond, but it was easy to see she didn't believe him either. The subtle shift of her eyes toward the mirror let him know she was weighing her options. And the half-step Aspen took away from him let him know he was going to lose her if he didn't give a little—and quickly. Just when he thought she was going to run, he saw her chin lift. *Bring it, baby. A fight means I have a chance, but if you walk away, we all lose.*

"Do my friends at Prairie Winds know you're trying to hang my ass out in the breeze? Because they are typically pretty protective." That was a fucking understatement if Nate had ever heard one, but he wasn't going to share how true he knew that statement to be. Yeah, Nate liked this little sub a lot. She was definitely going to challenge Mitch and Phoenix in ways they probably couldn't even imagine yet.

"Yes, they do. And I want you to know they have personally vetted the men on the other side of the mirror. Your safety is our first concern—*always*. Kent, Kyle, and Jax have all been involved in the discussion about your membership since the moment I saw you'd listed them as personal references. As you know, your membership at Prairie Winds only gets you in the door. Being a member of a collaborating club only guarantees you an interview."

From what he'd heard her relationship with the Wests and Jax, they were more like siblings than casual friends. And when he'd thought back on the conversations he'd had over the years with people in the lifestyle, there were some things sisters didn't feel like their brothers needed to know. And he was fairly certain, the details of their kink would be pretty high on the list.

Without missing a beat, she turned to the mirror, fisting her hands on her hips and narrowing her eyes. "They better not be behind that glass. I'm just telling you, I'm going to be damned mad if they are back there." Nate tried to suppress his smile, but he wasn't sure he'd succeeded. Damn if she hadn't just given him a loophole big enough for all of them to walk through.

"No, they are not on the other side of the glass. And as I said earlier, they have personally approved the men who are sitting in. It is important that we all know you are in safe hands." She nibbled on her bottom lip, and it took every bit of his control to refrain from correcting the nervous behavior. Aspen Andrews had no reason to be anxious around him, he was quickly coming to understand why the men who knew her were a protective bunch.

"Now, if you'll have a seat, we'll get down to business. I'm pleased you've already submitted your medical documentation—that's a big hurdle out of the way. Now we can focus on your needs and your limits list." Ordinarily, he challenged subs to be completely open about their needs and to expand their list, but that wasn't the case with Aspen. He suspected that her fantasy writing had revealed a lot more than she had intended. Her limit list was all but non-existent. If he turned her loose in the club on a regular play night, every wanna-be sadist in the club would be on her like white on rice.

"What's wrong with my list?" Again, she'd read the situation without him specifically stating he had an issue with what she'd submitted as a part of her application.

"Let's sit down. I want to make sure your experience here is everything you need it to be. But even more than that, I want to make sure you're safe. And to be perfectly honest, you wouldn't be safe with the list you submitted." For the first time, Nate saw a crack in her resolve. *That's right, love. There are Doms in this club who would eat you alive.*

JAX LOOKED OVER to where Kent and Kyle sat watching the large screen and shook his head. Hitting the mute button on the console, he voiced what he suspected was also going through his friends' minds. "How did we not see this coming? Christ, you gave her a five-year membership to Prairie Winds, but she's never actually played." The frown on Kyle's face told him they were in agreement—they'd all three dropped the ball where Aspen was concerned.

Kent's growl had both Jax and Kyle turning his way. "I should have known—of the three of us, I'm closest to her. Hell, I'd kick one of our member's ass if they failed a sub like this."

"So you're supposed to be the *be all and know all* for every submissive you come into contact with?" Tobi's voice from behind them surprised all three men. *Damn it, why didn't I lock the fucking door? I should have known her inner radar would zero in on something it shouldn't be aware of. I swear the woman is a damned trouble magnet.*

"Kitten, you aren't supposed to be in here." Kyle's voice was the usual mix of affection and annoyance Jax often noticed whenever he dealt with Tobi. The West brothers' wife wasn't at all what any of their friends had expected for the two Doms, but she had enchanted them from the moment they met her.

"I'm hungry, and there's no real food in the house...only ingredients." Jax coughed to cover his chuckle, but he hadn't fooled her. She shot him a quick glare before returning her attention to her husbands. "Millie took the kids to play group, and I'm not allowed to cook. I'll starve before she gets back." Jax was fighting back his laughter as her voice sounded more and more desperate. No one would describe Tobi West as incompetent in any way—except cooking. And where all things culinary were concerned, the little menace was downright dangerous.

Kent was on his feet in a heartbeat, and Jax didn't miss the knowing look he gave his brother. Jax knew his friends were convinced their wife was pregnant despite her insistence to the contrary. Personally, he thought the brothers were probably right, and Tobi was simply still in denial. During her first pregnancy, Kent and Kyle had practically smothered her, and Jax knew she wasn't anxious to repeat the restrictions they'd imposed the first time around.

"Come on, sweetness. I'll help you find something to eat. How about a nice bowl of fruit and tuna salad wrap?" *Geez, Kent, lay it on a little thicker with the healthy choices why don't you?* Tobi's groan was exactly what Jax expected, she wasn't going to be easily appeased by Kent's suggestions.

As soon as they'd stepped from the room, Jax looked at Kyle. "How long are you going to let her deny what is obvious to everyone?"

Kyle grinned even as he turned his attention back to the screen in front of him. "Kirk will be here later this afternoon. And if she doesn't want to cooperate, we'll bring in Brian." Kirk Evans and Brian Bennett were both obstetricians—they were also club members. The two men were married to the Prairie Winds office administrator. They'd been the only men who'd ever captured Regi's interest, but she'd fought the attraction for months before finally realizing how perfect they were for her. Kirk had a much softer approach which made him perfect for the first pitch with Tobi.

"So have the guys started a pool yet?" The men on the Wests' covert ops team usually had at least one pool going with regards to Tobi. The bets ranged from how long until her next spanking to her delivery date for the twins, and this wasn't something they'd let go by without some serious cash changing hands.

It took Kyle a few minutes to answer as he tried to focus on Aspen's answers to Nate's questions about limits, but he finally returned is attention to Jax. "Of course there's a pool. Hell, my guess is there's more than one. The local charities love us." A large percentage of the winner's *profits* went to their charity of choice. Those cash donations went a long way to endear the club to the locals.

Jax grinned. "I'll check and see if there are any good slots left. My favorite group needs new playground equipment."

Kyle rolled his eyes and laughed. "And we all know you will buy it for them even if you don't win." True enough, but it was still damned fun to win.

Chapter Six

PHOENIX LEANED FORWARD, riveted to the large window in front of him as he listened to Aspen explain why her hard limit list was practically nonexistent. Jesus, Joseph, and Mary, the woman was either far too naïve or dangerously reckless, and he wasn't sure which. Either way, she needed guidance—a lot of damned guidance in his opinion. Aspen was a unique contrast between intuitive and inexperience she fascinated him.

"It's a good thing there are two of us. Jesus, Joseph, and sweet Mother Mary, she's too fucking brave for her own good."

Phoenix nodded as he spoke, "You read my mind. Hell, I hope Nate and Taz drop a net over her until this plan comes together. If they turn her loose in the club, it'll be a feeding frenzy." He didn't intend to let that happen. There would be no unsupervised play for this little submissive whether she accepted them as her Masters or not.

"I suspect a guided tour of the lower dungeon will add to her hard limits in a big hurry. Seriously, she left on everything but any play involving blood? The damned woman is a tragedy waiting to happen. She needs a paddling that will serve as a reminder of her foolishness for several days." Mitch had been more understanding until he'd seen her confusion when Nate questioned her list. Phoenix agreed with Mitch's assessment—lighting up her beautiful ass would go a long way toward teaching her how serious they were about her safety. Hell, he thought his brothers' women were too cavalier about their safety, but they didn't hold a candle to the one he intended to claim.

"The tour is a great idea, but I've got a feeling the spanking might not turn out to be that much of a punishment." If he was honest, he wasn't sure there would be much aside from orgasm denial they'd be able to use as a punishment. "According to the Wests, she negotiated a five-year membership to the club, but she hasn't ever actually played there. I can't find any record of her at any other club, but she could have easily used another name." Or gone to one of the seedier clubs where names weren't an issue as long as you walked in with cash in your hand. Christ, just thinking about her in one of those clubs made his blood boil.

"Nate doesn't seem to be making much progress on the limits list. She's stubborn and too damned smart for her own good." Phoenix nodded in agreement but didn't comment. He'd seen how tenacious she could be. During the past year, they'd communicated almost daily, and he'd been convinced he knew Athena inside and out. But now, watching the woman who'd played that role to perfection as she answered intimate questions about her sexual preferences, Phoenix wondered how different his gaming nemesis was from the woman who'd just admitted to being a bit of an exhibitionist.

Mitch groaned. "Christ, it's killing me to listen to this. I want to drag her out of that damned office, tie her up in the play room and sink as deep as I can get into her heat. My brain is trying to listen, but my dick is shouting too loud for me to hear."

Yes, indeed. That was a plan Phoenix could definitely get behind. He hadn't been able to concentrate since she stepped out of her car in the parking lot. There had been a part of him that wasn't sure she'd actually show up, even as he'd tracked her through town using her cellphone location. *Why the hell hasn't Uncle Sam given her a secure device?* When they made her theirs, it was something they would change immediately.

"Everything's in place for tomorrow night. As long as this interview doesn't tank, we're good to go." Phoenix could hardly wait for the scene they'd set up. The entire evening would be a reenactment of the fantasy she'd written—or at least as close as they could make it without tapping into the local theatre department for sets and costumes. *Oh yeah, I can just imagine how that particular conversation would play out.* "I'm anxious to see which one of them show up." Phoenix nodded toward the small camera set up beside them. The video and audio feeds for the men at Prairie Winds were feeding directly to their control center outside Austin. They could talk to them via a separate audio link, but they'd muted the feed when Tobi walked in the room.

"I'd put my money on Jax. I can't see Kent or Kyle leaving Tobi if they think she's pregnant." When Phoenix raised a brow in question, Mitch grinned. "One of the guys on the team called me about the pool they've set up." His shrug made Phoenix laugh. "Hey, don't knock it. I actually got a couple of great dates and times; and the after school program I sponsor needs new basketball goals."

"When I was there I heard about the betting pools." Phoenix laughed. "Sounds like the local charities love it. Maybe we can get Nate to set up something like that here. There are a lot of worthy organizations in the area."

Once Nate wrapped up the discussion about the limits list, Phoenix watched him lean back in his chair as he studied Aspen. Nate intimidated most submissives; they found his careful consideration unnerving. But Aspen's years in the military had obviously exposed her to plenty of Alpha males because so far she hadn't appeared nervous in his presence. *It will be interesting to see if she is able to remain this distant when Mitch and I are involved.*

ASPEN HAD NEVER been so nervous in her entire life. Even the first few times she'd dodged surface to air fire, she hadn't been this apprehensive. Of course, she'd spent hundreds of hours in flight simulators training for those circumstances, and she was fairly certain that wasn't an option for this interview. Yeah, she could just picture how that particular simulator might work, asking all sorts of intimate questions…holy hell.

Nate Ledek now knew more about her sex life than her gynecologist. *Yeah and he'll likely be seeing more of your pink bits than your doc, too.* Damn, she'd like to smack her inner diva sometimes, the wench had a smart mouth and was as disrespectful as they came. And she liked to highjack Aspen's mouth every now and then, causing far more trouble than she was worth.

"I'd love to be able to listen in on those conversations you have with yourself. I suspect that is something your Masters will address in short order." Nate's voice was pitched lower, and there was something in the tone that brought her back to the moment in short order. She felt as if she'd been yanked back to the present and it took a minute to reorient herself to their conversation.

"Masters? As in more than one?" She hoped her voice hadn't given her away, but judging from the sly smile on his face it was probably safe to assume it had. After seeing so many of her friends in polyamorous relationships, she'd stopped wondering how she would ever be able to choose between the two men she'd secretly claimed as her own, and started wondering what it would be like to be between them.

Nate didn't answer, but his slow nod told her everything she needed to know. For a split second, she allowed herself to imagine Phoenix Morgan and Mitch Ames sitting on the other side of the glass. But she quickly pushed the thought aside. They didn't even know who she was, so why would they be there? Unless they were looking for a woman to share and her namesake had decided to intervene. After all, Athena was the goddess of war and strategy. Laughing at her own nonsense, Aspen refocused on the conversation with Nate.

WATCHING THROUGH THE scope of his rifle as Captain Andrews walked down the front steps of Montana's most popular kink club, Barry Orman didn't bother holding back his smile. He'd wondered how long it would be before she moved into position. *This is fucking perfect.*

There'd never been any doubt in his mind that she'd eventually run to Montana. Athena's on-line banter with the game developer and his friend had to have set some sort of world record for longest verbal foreplay in history. Barry hadn't been the only one who'd noticed, other gamers had been speculating about the relationship in private chat groups for months.

Everyone wondered which man she'd end up with. But, he'd had done his homework. He knew about her friends and their ménage lifestyles. Hell, he wasn't judging—what did he care if two dudes wanted to fuck the same woman? If they didn't care that nothing separated their cocks but a thin membrane, why should he?

No, Barry's goal was to make Phoenix Morgan suffer like he'd suffered—the fucker had stolen his future. Barry lost everything because of Morgan's God damned report. How the bastard managed to dig up all the dirt from Barry's past was still a mystery. Fucking hell, his parents had paid millions to suppress those police reports. But it wouldn't be a problem much longer.

As soon as Morgan fucked Captain Hot Pants, he'd be hooked and then Barry would set his plan into motion. Oh yeah, doing your homework definitely paid off in a lot of ways. He knew exactly how the Morgan brothers operated. There wasn't anything they wouldn't do for their women, and Phoenix wouldn't be any different. He'd change that report and sweep all the dirt back under the rug to get his woman back. *Oh, he'll get her back all right, one fucking piece at a time.*

ASPEN FELT HIM the minute she stepped out of the club. She hesitated briefly, turning back as if listening to someone inside even though Nate hadn't walked her all the way to the door. He'd been distracted by a phone call, and she'd just waved, then moved on alone. Even though she'd never met Phoenix's stalker, she recognized the energy immediately. Leaning back, pretending to sweep her heavy fall of hair off her shoulders as she pulled her sunglasses from her purse, Aspen took in her surroundings.

There were two different hilltops high enough to afford a sniper a clear shot, she'd check them both out later this evening. But there was something odd about the energy she was picking up, the danger seemed to be shifting from Phoenix to her. Whoever it was had a clear shot and had since the moment she'd stepped out onto the club's wide stone stairway. If he hadn't already dropped her, he wasn't going to...at least not yet. *Why would he be watching me? What purpose does that serve?*

Making her way to her car, Aspen made sure her body language didn't betray her awareness of his presence. She didn't want to do anything that would tipoff the stalker, it was hard to anticipate how he might react if he knew she'd felt him watching her. Once she'd gotten in her car, she started to shake and could barely get the key in the ignition. Reaching for her phone, she did what she'd done since she was a kid anytime something went wrong, she dialed her friends.

The three of them had once complained that she always called Kent, so she'd designed an app that rotated their number in random patterns. Today, it was Jax whose number appeared on her screen, and he answered on the first ring. "Hey beautiful, what's up?" His casual tone sounded a little more forced than usual, and it brought a smile to her face. No doubt he assumed she was calling about them allowing a couple of Doms to sit in on her interview. When she didn't answer immediately, he spoke again, this time, his voice filled with concern. "Aspen? Are you all right?"

Giving herself a mental shake when she heard Kyle and Kent's voices in the background, Aspen finally found her words. "Yes, well...yes and no. Someone is watching me. I just left Mountain Mastery, oh, you already knew that didn't you?" Suddenly her brain found another outlet for all the fear and anger she was feeling. "We're going to be having a long chat about that, too, don't think we're not. You guys are taking this over-protective brother routine too far; don't you think?"

"No, I don't think so." Jax's flat tone made it clear that particular topic was not open for discussion. *Pompous ass.* "What do you mean someone is watching you? Tell me, now." She heard Kyle cursing in the background and knew if she didn't get out of the parking lot quickly, Nate would be running out the front door to stop her. Once her pals dropped a net over her, she'd have a hell of a time getting out from under their thumbs.

Turning the key, her car purred to life. She heard Kyle's voice in the background, snarling, "Tell her to stay right where she is, or I'll paddle her ass myself." *Damn.* She hadn't even put the car in gear when it suddenly shut off. *Seriously?*

"Damnit, tell Micah to knock it off." Jax's business partner, Micah Drake was the only person Aspen knew, aside from Phoenix Morgan, with the computer skills to tap into her car's OnStar and shut it down. And since Phoenix didn't know who or where she was...Micah was a sure bet. "I am a big girl. How did he get my OnStar code anyway? Hell, never mind I don't want to know."

"Enough about your damned car. Stay right where you are and tell me about being watched. Your job isn't as damned secret as you think it is, which means there are any number of crazies who might be targeting you." *What?* She hadn't told them what her position entailed, and even though they knew who she worked for, they damned well shouldn't have any details. Sometimes their reach was just plain scary.

"I feel him. He's been tracking a guy I did a clearance for, but now I can feel him watching me. I just got scared...sorry I called and set off a panic. I'm good now." She tried to restart her car, but it was still dead. Slapping her hand down on the steering wheel, she cursed herself for calling them.

"I heard that. You did the right thing even if you don't think so. When was the last time your instincts were wrong?" He had her there. Truth was, her instincts were almost always spot on. Leaning her forehead against the steering wheel, Aspen tried to focus on the energy she'd felt just a few minutes before, but it was gone.

"He's gone. I've spotted two places where he could have been. I want to go check them out, but my car won't start. Let me do my job, Jax, you aren't playing fair. And if you hold me hostage I'm not going to call you the next time I'm scared or need help. I don't think this is about me, one of the men I did a clearance for has gained an *admirer*." Aspen knew she wasn't playing fair either, but there were times when the only way to fight a fire was with a fire of your own.

Jax muttered under his breath, and the next voice on the line was Kent's. "Sweetie, we're worried about you. Your instincts are terrific, but you also think you are invincible." *Not after the cluster fuck in St. Maarten, I don't.* "We almost lost you on that damned island, and we're not eager to repeat the experience. How worried would you be if one of us called you and said we were in some asshat's crosshairs?"

"Yeah, I get it. But disabling my car is a little over the top."

"If you hadn't been trying to leave after Jax told you to

stay put, it wouldn't have been necessary. Don't make me turn you over to Kyle, you already know how that will play out. Your next trip to the club wouldn't be simply a looky-loo visit." He had a point about the car, and he knew it. Damn, they could be exasperating. All three of them had the annoying habit of being right, but Kent didn't typically take such a hardline stance with her. Threatening to turn her over to Kyle was just plain mean.

Lifting her face from its resting place, Aspen groaned. "You called Nate?"

"No, we called Taz—and he called Nate. Look behind you." Aspen turned around just as the grill of a huge truck filled her rearview mirror. *Well, shit.*

Chapter Seven

PHOENIX WAS ABOUT ready to tear Nate's office apart. While destroying the club's office wouldn't accomplish anything, it might ease the tension that had been threatening to erupt for the past twenty-four hours. It had been bad enough hearing the playback of Aspen's phone call to Jax yesterday. Despite her later protests, the fear in her voice had been much too easy to hear. The only thing that had kept him from running out the front door of Mountain Mastery was knowing Nate and Taz were already moving into position. He and Mitch had planned to return to the ranch to pick up the last of the props for tonight's scene, but Aspen's call scrapped those plans.

One call to Kip solved their problem, his youngest brother reluctantly agreed to deliver everything they needed for tonight's scene. Kip had been tired and damned cranky. Phoenix wasn't sure if it had been the actual process of first "collection day" or the stress of dealing with Calamity. Whatever it was, Kip set it aside quickly when he heard what had taken place the day before in the club's lot. The only question his younger brother had asked was, "Do you know who the stalker is?" When Phoenix gave him a short list of possibilities, he'd simply reminded Phoenix to watch his back before ending the call.

Mitch paced the room as he spoke, "We found evidence of someone sitting on the hill south of the club. It was the place where Aspen indicated she'd felt the strongest energy." Mitch shook his head and smiled. "I'm telling you now, this woman is going to keep us on our toes. Hell, her damned gaming name was dead on. Her instincts are sharper than hell; she's doing her goddess namesake proud."

"I've listened to the tape of the phone call several times, and I keep coming back to the reason she's here. The first thing she mentions is that someone she'd done a clearance on was being stalked? Do you think that's why she's here?" It was almost beyond his imagination—he'd never had anybody but family put themselves on the line for him.

"The fantasy she wrote is a window directly into her soul. Remember, in the beginning, she described Athena as a protector. I believe the phrase was *a champion of other victims*. Personally, I think that is just the first of many things we'll discover are clues to the core of Aspen Andrews. Remember, she said Athena had run out of places to hide—I'd say Aspen's subconscious knew we were closing in on her. She doesn't appear to be aware that we're on to her, but she had to know it was just a matter of time."

"We'll know soon enough. It looks like everything downstairs is almost ready." They'd been standing in Nate's office looking down over the club's main room through the large glass window. From the main room, all anyone could see was their silhouettes, Phoenix loved the specially treated glass and planned to utilize it when he remodeled his suite in the ranch's main house. With the touch of a button, the glass could be changed to anything from clear to completely reflective, it was a great piece of technology.

"I can hardly wait to peel the layers of clothing from

her. Damn, I thought we'd done a great job with the costumes, but the treasure trove Gracie brought put everything I'd put together look pathetic." No doubt he'd be hearing about Kip's wasted effort for days, but his younger brother's complaints would fall on deaf ears. Phoenix knew Nate had already extended Kip a personal invitation to tonight's special event. And even though he didn't know why—everyone knew Nate Ledek's actions were never random. If he'd made the effort to call Kip personally—there was a reason, and probably a damned important one.

"Gracie said Tobi helped with the costumes for the subs. And she was—and I quote, 'pissed seven ways to Sunday' that she wasn't allowed to fly up here with Jax, Micah, and Gracie. If she really is pregnant, her Masters will have their hands full. She knows they won't spank her until well after the baby is born and she'll rack up punishment points like a champ until then." Micah always had the same grin on his face when he spoke about Tobi. Phoenix didn't even want to think about how challenging she could be if she was deliberately acting out. Hell, the woman was a spitfire when she wasn't even trying to challenge her husbands.

GRACIE SAT ON the bed watching Aspen pace the length of the large room. She knew Nate and Taz had insisted Aspen stay in one of the club's large guest suites last night instead of returning to the hotel where she'd checked in. After the scare she'd had yesterday, Gracie was sure any protest Aspen had waged had been token at best.

"You'd better save some of that energy, I can assure

you you're going to need it." Gracie didn't even try to keep the amusement out of her voice. She'd met Aspen a couple of times at Prairie Winds, but they hadn't spent much time together until this evening. Tasked with helping Aspen get ready for tonight's reenactment of her fantasy, she'd dressed the woman in several layers before Aspen's eyes lit with understanding.

"I can't believe Nate is orchestrating this. Do they do this for all submissives applying for membership? I mean, it has to be a tremendous expense." Aspen finally settled on the other side of the bed and looked at Gracie.

"First of all, this has been a group effort. Nate isn't the only one involved, but that isn't my story to tell. In answer to your question, no they don't do this for all applicants. I'm sure you can see how expensive that would be. But if you're being honest with yourself, you know you aren't just another submissive applying for membership. You are for all intents and purposes a member of a very special family."

Gracie wanted to laugh when Aspen simply blinked at her in confusion. The woman really was adorable, as well as gorgeous. One of the things she noticed while helping Aspen with her makeup and hair was the young woman's complete lack of self-awareness. Her long blonde hair and bright green eyes topped off a curvy figure Gracie would bet got her more second looks than she knew. But even more important was her lack of understanding about how important she was to the people around her.

"My husband certainly considers you a member of his family, and I know Kent and Kyle do as well. I think you'll have a better understanding of how important you are to people at the end of this evening." Aspen continued to blink, looking like a baby owl and it made Gracie smile.

"The only thing I'm asking is that you keep an open mind and an open heart. Accept the gifts you're given tonight...and I'm not talking about things you hold in your hand. No, these gifts will be far more precious. These gifts are held in the heart so they can never be taken away from you."

For the first time, Gracie saw understanding dawn in Aspen's sea green eyes as they went glassy with unshed tears. Before she could respond, a heavy knock at the door made Aspen jump. Jax and Micah stepped into the room, their eyes softening when they saw Gracie sitting on the edge of the bed. Jax stepped in front of her, while Micah settled behind her back and wrapped his arms around her and pulling her against his chest.

Jax smiled at the two of them before turning to Aspen. "I'm your escort for the first part of this evening, sweetness. Once you've been handed off to the Doms running the show, I'll back off, but I won't ever be far away. If you need me, you just have to call out my name, and I'll be beside you in an instant."

Aspen moved so fast Gracie had barely registered her shift before the woman threw herself into Jax's arms. "You're the best, you know that? I love you to pieces, even if you are bossy and annoying sometimes." Gracie laughed out loud, and Jax gave her a warning look that didn't hold any heat at all.

Micah leaned forward whispering against the sensitive shell of her ear. "I get you all to myself for a little while, baby. And I'm very much looking forward to capturing you in the chaos so make sure you stay where I put you when we get downstairs." Gracie was looking forward to spending time with Micah, also. He'd been out of town for business on and off during the past few weeks, and she'd missed him. And knowing her *planner* husband, he had something special all lined up for her...and she could hardly wait.

She had two wonderful children with these men, and even the day-to-day strain of keeping their household together hadn't dimmed her desire for them. One of the things she loved most about the two of them was how they never distinguished between the kids despite the fact it was obvious which man was the biological parent. Deaga definitely belonged to Micah, her sandy blonde hair and crystal blue eyes made her the spitting image of her Daddy. But her sweet Dougy was McDonald through and through. Even as a baby, he was already so tall for his age he wasn't registering on the charts. His easy smile and deep blue eyes were topped off with jet black hair and always drew the ladies to him in the same way she'd seen them flock to Jax. Douglas Drake McDonald was definitely going to be a heartbreaker.

It would serve Jax right to have a son just like him, but honestly, Micah hadn't done a thing to deserve the strong-willed Deaga. Their daughter was brilliant, but the little hellion had definitely inherited her mama's stubborn streak. But the thing that terrified all three of her parents was Deaga's devotion to Tobi West. The little girl idolized all things Tobi and Lilly. It was downright terrifying. Tobi might be Gracie's best friend, but just thinking about raising a child like her was almost enough to send Gracie into a panic attack.

Micah tightened his arms around her and spoke softly against her ear. "What has you teetering on the edge of a meltdown, baby? There is no reason to worry about the children, they love your mother." He was right, and Gracie was grateful her mother had been willing to return to

Austin to watch her only grandchildren.

"I was just thinking about Deaga's hero-worship of Tobi and how much it scares me." She felt more than heard him chuckling behind her.

"Baby, I will grant you that our beautiful daughter thinks the sun rises and sets on both Tobi and Lilly. But I'm honestly worried she is simply taking notes on what doesn't work so she doesn't repeat their mistakes. What she'll come up with on her own is likely going to be more refined and far more dangerous."

Gracie gasped and wondered if all the blood had drained from her face because Jax was suddenly standing in front of her, concern clearly written in his expression. "What did you say to her? Hell, she's as pale as a fucking ghost all of the sudden."

"I simply told her that our daughter is using Tobi and Lilly as points of reference rather than planning to emulate them." Micah's hands slid inside the low cut dress she was wearing, his fingers rolling her nipples back and forth, the pressure increasing each time he changed direction.

"*Cariño*, don't worry. There are three of us to watch after her." Even though her eyes were beginning to be more unfocused as desire pulsed through her, Gracie saw Jax's attention shift to Micah. "Stop tormenting our sub, I want to enjoy some time inside her later when I don't have to worry about who's watching. Worrying about our preschool princess and dapper-diaper Don Juan isn't what I want her thinking about."

This time, Micah laughed out loud. "Agreed. I'll see if I can wind her up a bit, but don't wait too long to join the party. I have been away from her far too much lately, and I'm looking forward to making up for lost time."

Jax snorted then turned to Aspen. "Let's go, sweetness.

Things to do and a sub to do them with. Let's get this party started."

CAILA COOPER WAS looking forward to getting some serious stress relief tonight. Spending a couple of days in the Morgan's barn with Kip had nearly pushed her over the edge. God in heaven, was there a more exasperating man in the entire world? He'd nearly tripped over himself several times trying to keep from brushing up against her. She felt as though she'd fallen through Alice's looking glass and everything was backwards...Kip was the one being clumsy, not her. And him nearly falling trying to steer clear of her instead of her tumbling over things in her mad dash to get closer to him was certainly new.

He needn't worry. She'd given up on Kip Morgan. There were other men out there, and she planned to find one tonight. She'd been thrilled when Master Nate called to invite her to the special event the club was hosting. Caila had been a member of another club close to campus when she heard about Mountain Mastery. She'd scheduled an interview with the club's owner and five minutes into her interview with Nate Ledek, Caila had known she'd found a new club home.

Caila had only attended one open night so she'd been surprised by Master Nate's call. During her interview, she'd confessed her need to set aside her lifelong crush on Kip, and it had been the only time she'd seen Master Nate's expression flicker with something she couldn't identify...recognition, perhaps? The change was so fleeting, she wasn't sure it had even been real, so she pushed it to the back of her mind.

Standing beside another woman whose Dom hovered nearby, Caila was starting to question her decision to attend when a warm hand settled on top of her shoulder. Warm and huge. "Breathe, little vet. You look like you are about ready to bolt." She turned to see a man who looked so much like Master Nate she knew they must be brothers. "My name is Master Taz. I'm Nate's better looking brother." The man was huge and would have been intimidating if not for his welcoming smile.

One of the women beside her squealed and launched herself at the man who'd just introduced himself as Taz. "Oh, Master Taz, I'm so happy to see you. How have you been? We've missed you at Prairie Winds."

One of the men who'd been standing nearby practically growled at his wayward sub. "Gracie. You know the rules; I swear to God you have been spending too much time with Tobi." Caila wasn't sure who these people were, but it was more than obvious they were all friends.

When she started to take a step back, the hand that had been on her shoulder a few seconds earlier returned. "Don't move, sub." She felt her eyes widen in surprise, and she worried she'd gotten into trouble without even trying. Caila was much more at ease with her four-legged friends. They didn't laugh when she tripped over thin air, and she'd never had a single one call her Calamity, either.

"Breathe, sweetness." Caila let out the breath she hadn't even realized she was holding and looked up at the man who'd been watching over the dark-haired woman he'd pulled out of Master Taz's arms. "Taz, are you going to introduce us to this lovely lady?"

"Absolutely. I think she was getting ready to make a run for it, so having a few friends would probably be helpful. I'm happy to introduce a new member to a sub I don't think will lead her into trouble." Gracie made an exaggerated gesture feigning innocence. Her Dom shook his head but didn't say anything.

After Taz had made the introductions, Gracie pulled her aside while the men chatted nearby. "I know there aren't many subs here, but this reenactment doesn't require many subs. If you don't have a Dom, you're going to be getting a lot of attention. If you aren't comfortable with that, you need to tell Master Taz now."

"I'll be fine. I'm hoping to find a play partner. I've...well, I've recently given up on a guy I'd thought would eventually be my future. I held on to that dream far longer than I should have." Gracie watched her closely, and Caila worried her new friend saw more than she should. Luckily, before Gracie could ask any questions, Master Nate stepped into the room letting everyone know things were about to begin.

When he'd called to invite her to this special event, Nate had briefly explained they were reenacting the fantasy a new member had written in her application. Caila had breathed a sigh of relief, grateful she'd declined to write a fantasy. It had been their conversation about leaving the section blank that led to her confession about Kip. Now, it seemed the embarrassment she'd felt while talking about her girlish crush paled in comparison to what the woman being led up onto the stage was going to endure.

The woman was about her Caila's height, but as far as she could tell that's where the similarities ended. *Damn, she's stacked. Why couldn't I have gotten breasts like those?* The pretty blonde must have been wearing several layers of clothing, damn, she looked like she was sweltering under the stage lights. The woman was blindfolded and being hustled toward the edge of the stage by what Caila assumed was supposed to be a horny bunch of ancient thugs. Hell, being blindfolded and manhandled would probably make her sweat, too. When Caila realized she'd been seeing herself in the other woman's position instead of listening, she tried to focus on the scene playing out in front of her.

By the time, she realized her neighbor was one of the men strapping the woman to a St. Andrew's cross, she was looking for the exit. This was going to be way more information about Phoenix Morgan than she wanted to know, but her eyes kept returning to the stage. Caila stood mesmerized, unable to move, even when she knew she should. The sound of fabric shredding sent a flood of heat racing over her skin. She hadn't been able to suppress the shudder that worked up her spine and cringed when male chuckles surrounded her. *Terrific.*

Chapter Eight

ASPEN'S MIND REELED as she tried to make sense of what she was seeing. It looked like someone had inserted a cross-section of a castle into the large open area at one end of the club's main playroom. The décor was so eerily close to what she'd described in her fantasy it stole her breath. She froze halfway up the steps, but Jax obviously wasn't in the mood to delay his own gratification because he simply wrapped his enormous hands around her waist and lifted her up the last few steps.

Once she was on the stage everything around her faded into the background. She forgot how hot she was in the layers of clothing she wore; despite the fact she felt like she was being roasted alive. Blinking in an effort to bring the large room back into focus, Aspen let her eyes dart around the room. The club certainly wasn't filled to capacity, but there were more people standing around the stage than she'd expected. Between Nate and Jax, she'd gotten bits and pieces of what was planned. But now that she saw how they'd managed to transform the stage area into an ancient castle, she knew how close they'd played their cards to their chests.

She heard a commotion at the back of the club and felt adrenaline begin to course through her veins. Aspen looked for Jax just as he faded into the shadows at the back of the stage. Remembering the promise he'd made upstairs, she knew he wasn't going far. The security she felt knowing he was nearby made all the difference, it was the only thing keeping her from running from the room. The entire production was overwhelming, to say the least. Someone had gone to a lot of trouble to set this up, and Aspen was becoming more and more uncomfortable not knowing who was responsible.

By the time she turned her attention back to the stage, men dressed in what looked like ancient military garb had rushed up the steps and quickly surrounded her. They said little as they restrained her and tied a silk blindfold over her eyes. She smiled to herself at their use of fine silk, not period appropriate, but she was grateful for their lapse. They held her arms tight—but far from the punishing grip she'd described in her writing, obviously they didn't want to risk hurting her. They started to hustle her from where she'd been standing, but hadn't made it off the stage when Aspen felt the men halt abruptly. A few seconds later a commanding voice ordered them to release her and to step back.

Aspen almost missed the first brush of air as someone moved past her. They'd been close…very close, but hadn't actually touched her. Her senses were on high alert, but she stood perfectly still waiting for some clue who she was dealing with. Warm breath against her ear startled her, but when she started to step back, she found herself plastered against a second captor. A steel chest pressed against her back and another was so close she could feel the pressure against her peaked nipples despite the layers of clothing she wore. She'd been worried about sweating beneath the layers, but that concern was quickly being eclipsed by arousal.

Her body was reacting to the men surrounding her,

and they hadn't even touched her. Her fight or flight responses were shouting that she should be afraid, but the energy pulsing around her didn't feel threatening. She felt controlled, even though they weren't touching her.

Aspen reminded herself there wasn't any real danger, after all, this was a staged production, and Jax was nearby. Master Nate wouldn't let anything happen to her either, his club had a spotless record when it came to safety. But all of those facts began to fade with four small words. The man in front of her leaned forward again, this time pressing closer and circling her ear with the tip of his tongue. "Athena, finally we meet."

Aspen gasped and felt her knees fold out from under her. A strong arm wrapped around her waist pulling her back against a rock hard chest holding her upright until she was able to lock her knees. Good Lord, what had she been thinking? During her years in the military, she'd never forgotten to lock her knees. It was a testament to how unnerved she was that she'd lost control and nearly fallen. "Careful, little goddess. We aren't following your script verbatim, but we certainly aren't going to allow you to be injured either."

Once she was steady, his arm fell away, and she felt him step away from her. The next time he spoke it was obvious his words were intended for the benefit of the entire room. Holy hell, the man's voice almost echoed off the walls, and she fought the urge to wince at the booming noise so close to her ear. "A goddess, indeed. Stunning despite the armor she wears."

Aspen hadn't recognized his voice when the words had been spoken so intimately, but now it's familiarity stunned her. "Mitch?"

She tried to turn, but the man in front of her grabbed

her upper arms halting her movement. "Play your part, little goddess. You are already in enough trouble for leading us on a merry chase for months." This time, his words were spoken so close to her ear the warm rush of air against the sensitive skin sent a bolt of lightning directly to her sex. Liquid warmed the folds of her sex, and the throbbing of her clit made her wish she could rub her legs together to ease the ache.

Oh shit, if Mitch was behind her that meant Phoenix Morgan was the man standing in front of her. *How did they figure out who I am? Damn, I was so careful.* She'd wanted to watch him play, not be the toy he was playing with…or had she? Each time she'd replayed the fantasy in her mind, the two of them had been the men who'd claimed her. Aspen had always tried to be as honest with herself, and she was with others, but it was obvious she'd kept her head in the sand this time.

Phoenix's voice filled the air as he asked if she'd put on the extra layers to prevent being dragged through the streets naked and she answered yes. They'd stayed as close to her fantasy as possible, and a part of her was grateful she had some idea what was coming. Having written it, she wasn't completely in the dark. A nervous giggle bubbled up at the absurdity of her unintentional pun, and she felt one of the men bite down lightly on the lobe of her ear. "We'll see how funny it is when you're under our lash. How will the goddess of strategy handle the strokes she's earned?"

As nervous as she was, some of her anxiety was eased because she knew what was supposed to come next. While being naked in public sounded good on paper, she was suddenly worried about being judged…but in the end, her body's need to cool down won out. As the layers were stripped away, all she felt was relief. *Fuck the costumes, I'm going to pass out from the heat.* Aspen felt herself wobble again and fought the urge to reach up and wipe the sweat from her forehead.

Following the script, they striped her of the extra layers, stopping when they reached the light-weight peplos she wore over her linen undergarments. The underwear she'd been given might be made of fine linen, but that was where the historical accuracy ended. The tiny scraps of fabric held together by silk ribbons hardly qualified for undergarments in her view.

Their soft words of praise fell on deaf ears when they began caressing her through the thin fabric. Mitch's hands slid from her shoulders to her wrists, shackling them and pulling them over her head. The position caused her back to arch, and pushed her large breasts out as if they were seeking Phoenix's attention. He didn't disappoint, his large hands cupped her breasts, and his fingers rolled both nipples until they were tight, throbbed, and begged for more.

Mitch moved her wrists so he could easily hold both with one hand. His free hand slid under her hair, and his fingers threaded through the long strands. He tightened his fingers until Aspen gasped at the exquisite feeling of straddling the line between pleasure and pain. When he pulled her head back, he turned her face to his, and whispered, "We'll push you, little goddess, don't think this entire scene is going to play out as written. Keeping you a bit off balance will be a good lesson—one of many I expect we'll be teaching you." His lips pressed against hers and she felt herself tumbling headfirst into the temptation.

The kiss was a journey. What started as a sweet distraction, turned into nothing short of a passion-filled message spoken directly to her heart. She'd known he was interested in her when they were in St. Maarten, but circumstances kept them from reconnecting after she was released from the hospital. Was this the second chance she always believed fate gave the worthy? *And what on Earth makes you think you are worthy?* Hell's bells and seashells, maybe he was the one who's worthy and she was just along for the ride.

MITCH WASN'T SURE he was going to have the patience to finish the scene before stripping Aspen bare and pushing himself balls deep into her luscious body. She was indeed the very picture of a Goddess. Her lush curves, cascading blonde curls, and satiny skin were pushing his control to its very limit. He could already smell her arousal and the pure ambrosia was making his cock twitch in anticipation. She'd looked so surprised when he ended the kiss and discovered the blindfold had been removed. He'd nearly laughed since it had been one of the last elements of her fantasy they planned to play out as written. From this point forward the scene was their response—their answer to the challenge her fantasy laid down to any Dom who read it.

He secured her to the St. Andrew's cross as Phoenix reminded her they intended to punish her for all the months they'd spent chasing her. Mitch saw the moment she realized they'd left her clothes intact. He fought his smile because they had no intention of leaving her covered. *Oh no, little sub, you've played us long enough. Now it's our turn to call the shots.*

Mitch gave Phoenix a thumbs up when he was satisfied with the bindings, then he stepped to the side where he'd have a better view. He'd gotten the first kiss, but Phoenix was going to unwrap the package and Mitch certainly didn't want to miss the show. For the first time since they'd started planning this evening's scene, Mitch was confident in the outcome. He'd worried they were taking things too far—too quickly, but the way she'd submitted to his kiss had given him hope they were on the right path.

Phoenix stepped in front of Aspen, the back of his finger sliding slowly down the side of her face. Mitch watched as goosebumps followed Phoenix's finger as it trailed all the way down the side of her neck. By the time his finger stopped at the top of her rounded breast, Aspen was panting and the flush of desire painted her cheeks a lovely shade of pink. "You're far too lovely to hide beneath such an ill-fitting frock, milady."

His hands fisted in the top layer of clothing and a quick jerk filled the air with the sound of tearing fabric. The soft linen gave way easily and after a few more quick pulls, all her clothing lay in tatters around her feet. Her eyes were impossibly wide, and had turned a deep shade of green as they filled with desire, making Mitch grateful they hadn't blindfolded her again—yet.

PHOENIX LOOKED AT the naked woman bound to the cross, and for several seconds his mind was completely devoid of everything except an insane urge to claim her. But those selfish thoughts were soon overcome by his appreciation for her beauty. *She's fucking gorgeous.* He already loved her mind, he'd gotten to know how she thought during the months he'd spent chatting with her. They'd bantered back and forth—disagreeing at times, but always respecting the other's opinion. He'd fallen in love with her before they'd even met face to face. The beautiful package her sweet heart, sharp wit, and intelligent mind were wrapped in was a bonus.

It was going to be hard to reorient his thinking, to integrate what he was learning about Aspen Andrews into what he already knew about Athena. She'd been Athena in his mind for so long, she'd almost become larger than life. It was easy to forget you were dealing with a real person when all of your communication was on-line. But now, looking at her voluptuous curves and full breasts, all he could think about was how good it was going to feel when he finally had her beneath him.

Tracing the thin scar running up her side with the tip of his finger, he leaned down to press a kiss against the narrow white line. It was damned humbling to realize how easily he could have lost her without ever knowing she belonged to him. "Remind me to thank Dr. Barnes when I meet her. From what I've been told she saved your life; she's my new hero." He didn't want to ignore the mark on her lovely skin, but he didn't want her self-conscious of it either.

"We're going to get your punishment out of the way first. Then we'll move to a private room for the next part of this little *meet and greet*." Phoenix's words seemed to take her by surprise and her pupils dilated, a look of desire moving over her expression. "I love the fact you aren't trying to hide how much you want us. Lying will never work out well for you, my sweet Athena." Using the Greek goddess's pretty moniker was a wonderful pet name for her, a way for him to pay homage to their past.

Mitch moved in front of her at Phoenix's nod, dragging the silk blindfold slowly over the tops of her breasts. He let the edge of the fabric brush erotically against the lower slope, dancing against her areolas before catching on her tightly peaked nipples. The hemmed edge of the silk was suspended for several heartbeats as it lifted her nipples invitingly upward. He smiled at her soft gasp as the pressure finally released and her breasts bounced free.

In his peripheral view, Mitch watched Phoenix pick up the soft flogger he planned to use, keeping it out of her view. Mitch continued to tease her with kisses and the scarf for several minutes, by the time he slid the blindfold back in place she was mewing softly, her head falling back on her shoulders. *Perfect.*

THE FLOGGER HE'D chosen would bring the blood to the surface, a tempting preview of things to come. But Phoenix didn't intend to give her the orgasm he knew her body was going to crave. He'd keep her release just beyond her reach, making it all the more intense when it was finally given. Phoenix had been a Dom for years, sinking into the role and learning everything he could about the dynamics of sexual dominance. He'd approached the study of becoming a sexual Dominant in the same way he learned anything else that interested him—complete immersion.

During their long conversations, he and Mitch discovered they'd both been fascinated with the emotional gratification they felt when a submissive responded to what they could give them. The trust between a Dom and his sub becoming almost tangible during a scene. The power exchange fulfilled everyone involved, if it was handled right. He'd had vanilla sex, but had never found the same level of connection with a woman who wasn't a submissive. If he wasn't calling the shots in the bedroom, it just wasn't going to work. "What's your safe word, sweet Athena?"

"Red, Sir." Her voice was already becoming airy, and Phoenix was pleased she was falling quickly into the perfect mindset for this part of the scene. He'd enjoyed their short journey back in time, but he hadn't been sorry to cut that portion short in favor of getting back to the here and now. There was no doubt their audience was enjoying this portion more as well.

"Perfect. Don't forget you can also use yellow if you need a break. We'll stop and talk it through, but I'm not promising we won't continue. Do you understand?" Phoenix knew she was inexperienced in the lifestyle, but she'd spent enough time with Doms to recognize the shift in his tone.

When she simply nodded, Mitch gave her ass a sharp swat, and she stuttered, "Yes, Sir. I understand." The sweet tone of her voice sent a rush of blood straight to his cock. Damn, he hoped like hell he got through this without coming in his leathers like a horny, out of control teenager.

Phoenix glanced to the side and caught a glimpse of a woman who reminded him of Caila Cooper despite the dark wig she was wearing. He did a double take, but she stepped behind the man she'd been talking to, putting her out of his view. Phoenix might not have gotten a good enough look to be sure it was his lifelong neighbor, but he'd gotten a good look at her clothing. As soon as he turned the scene over to Mitch, he'd signal Kip. It didn't matter how much Kip protested, Phoenix knew his youngest brother was more interested in Calamity than he admitted.

Returning his attention to Aspen, Phoenix trailed the soft strands of the flogger down the slope of her shoulder tracing invisible lines around the outer perimeter of each breast. The goosebumps that followed the leather strips let him know how wonderfully her body was responding to the stimulation. "Your skin is amazing. Soft and the most beautiful shade of ivory I've ever seen. I'm not sure Mother Nature has given us anything to match this magnificent shade."

Pulling the flogger away from where he'd been swirling it softly over her breasts, he smiled at Mitch before leaning down to run his tongue in slow circles around each nipple then blowing soft puffs of air over them. They drew up into impossibly tight peaks, and he smiled at their perfection. He couldn't wait to clamp them, letting a fine gold chain strung with faceted gems dangle between the rose colored tips. Oh yeah, emeralds that matched her eyes would be perfect.

"Let's see how many shades of pink we can turn these beautiful breasts before you are begging us to let you come." He'd already started the subtle lashes that she probably thought was nothing more than brushes of the leather strips. The goal was to build so gradually Aspen wasn't aware of the shift in intensity, because despite what he'd told her, this wasn't really a punishment—at least not in the traditional sense. She hadn't agreed to be their sub, and there hadn't been any discussion of rules prior to her evasion, so they had no real claim for punishment. But that didn't mean they weren't going to push the rule as far as they could and use it for their scene. She'd get the orgasm her body was already clamoring for—eventually. The entire production would be a reward—eventually.

Chapter Nine

*D*AMN IT, A *dead donkey would have seen Phoenix Morgan looking my direction before I did.* Phoenix looked right at her and for a couple of seconds, she thought he'd recognized her. *Why didn't Master Nate tell me he was part of the star attraction tonight?* Caila had ducked behind the Dom trying to talk her into scening with him. He'd seemed pleasant enough, but she hadn't felt any spark, so she'd politely declined. Turning to make her way out of the room, Caila came to an abrupt halt when a large hand wrapped around her upper arm. "Where do you think you're going, pet?"

Looking up at Master Nate threatened to topple her over backward. When she tried to take a step back to ease the strain on her neck, he shook his head no. With no effort at all, Master Nate picked her up and set her on the bar behind her. "I'm still waiting for you to answer my question, little one." Caila fought the urge to roll her eyes, but all things considered, she knew exactly where that would lead. One of the things she'd learned was Doms and cowboys were both relentless...*and cowboys who are Doms are stubborn as hell.*

Deciding honesty was her best bet, Caila sighed. "I was leaving, Sir. You didn't mention that Phoenix Morgan would be here. He's my neighbor, and I'm not comfortable..."

She didn't get to finish because he pressed his finger against her lips. "Be very careful what you say next, little vet. You'll be punished for lying to yourself just as quickly as you will be for lying to me—and you're getting awfully close to doing both."

When she nodded her understanding, he continued. "What you are telling me is you don't trust Master Phoenix to follow the strict non-disclosure agreement he signed when he joined the club. His agreement was exactly like the one you signed, pet."

She felt the blood drain from her face, that wasn't what she'd meant at all. Shaking her head, she struggled to find the right words. "No. I mean, no, Sir. That wasn't what I meant. I'm just not sure it's a good idea for us both to be here. We're neighbors. It just seems wrong."

"You should know that we have several members who are closely related. They love and respect one another enough to play in different areas when they are uncomfortable. Are you telling me you aren't willing to respect Master Phoenix's kinks, and you don't believe he'll respect yours?" Holy crap on a cactus, when he said it like that, it sounded awful. She wished the teak bar she was sitting on would slide apart and drop her into oblivion. Embarrassed didn't even begin to cover it. Caila hadn't thought that far ahead, she'd simply reacted. And if she was being honest, it wasn't Phoenix who worried her, it was Kip, because where you found Phoenix you usually found his younger brother.

"I'm sorry, Sir. I didn't think of it that way…nor was I trying to be disrespectful."

"Then perhaps you'd like to tell me what the *real* problem is." She wasn't fooled by his conciliatory tone, after all, in her line of work she was surrounded by Alpha males all the time...Caila knew an order when she heard one.

"I just need to put some distance between myself and the Morgans...well, not professional distance, but personal distance. I've made a fool of myself forever, and I'm done with it. It's just too embarrassing." She fought back the tears burning the backs of her eyes and hoped he didn't see the pain piercing her heart.

When Caila tried to look away, Master Nate used his fingers to grip her jaw and turn her to face him. "Thank you for finally trusting me with the truth, sweetness. Remember, there are times in life we have to suffer through some embarrassment in order to get to our goal." She took a deep breath and nodded.

After years of banging her head against a wall, she'd finally been forced to admit defeat. Changing her goal hadn't been easy, but she'd decided to move on. Despite her unease, Caila decided to stay. If she was going to find the relief she'd come for, she'd need to suck it up and find a play partner. She started to scoot off the bar, but the hand Master Nate had on her thigh tightened in warning. "Don't move, pet."

The club's owner looked to his left and when Caila followed his gaze she was surprised to see his brother standing beside them. Taz Ledek was also enormous, but his smile softened his features and made him look more approachable than the stern man who'd lifted her to the bar as if she weighed nothing at all. "Master Taz, this little sub was going to cut and run, but I believe we've talked through that particular challenge. She doesn't have a play partner. Are you free?" *What?* She'd never played in a real club before, so someone a little less experienced would be better, right? Her only experience was a play party hosted by a couple of college friends. *Holy shit, Sherlock. I might have exaggerated my experience on my application a little…okay, a lot.*

NATE WATCHED CAILA'S pulse at the base of her neck accelerate until he worried her heart was going to beat right out of her chest. He already knew she'd greatly exaggerated her play experience; it hadn't taken long in the interview to figure it out. Ordinarily, he'd have sent her on her way for that particular offense, but her mention of Kip Morgan had caught his interest. The younger man was a member of the club, and although Nate knew he wasn't a serious player, he seemed to have an almost innate knowledge about what women wanted.

And now, watching her closely as her mind scrambled to find a way to escape, Nate had to fight back his smile. He'd been watching her from the back of the room when she realized she'd caught Phoenix's attention. Even with her blonde hair hidden beneath the dark wig, her dainty features made her hard to miss. She'd panicked and tried to run, but he'd made it across the room in time to stop her. He'd been surprised when he wrapped his hand around her upper arm. The muscles hidden under her soft flesh rippled beneath his fingertips, the woman was obviously in good shape. Her muscle tone was well hidden in the loose fitting dress she was wearing, but she wouldn't be covered for long.

For the first time in a long time, Nate wished he had a sub of his own. But this little inexperienced beauty's heart belonged to the man leaning casually behind the bar. Challenging her to be honest with him was easy. Caila was naturally submissive and her desire to please him ensured her compliance. She was trying desperately to convince herself she was finished with Kip Morgan, but Nate wasn't buying it. In fact, Nate would bet it was Kip rather than Phoenix who was the reason she'd been desperately trying to finagle a way out of the club without getting her pretty little ass in a pinch.

Nate didn't usually play match-maker, but this little sub was definitely in need of some help. He and Taz hadn't been blessed with a little sister, so maybe they'd adopt Caila as their little sis with a kink. Taz had moved into place beside him, but he was sure the little subbie in front of him hadn't noticed their little chat was being observed. Nate also made sure Caila didn't see Kip Morgan standing nearby, because he was planning to test her commitment to staying away from the man she obviously wanted.

KIP LEANED WITH is back against a door behind the bar and watched Nate stop a dark-haired woman who appeared to have been trying to leave. He couldn't see her face but there was something vaguely familiar about her movements that caught his eye. Since he was standing almost directly behind where Nate had set her on the bar, Kip couldn't hear their conversation, but it was obvious she being called out for trying to walk out. *Poor little sub, if she's on Nate's shit list, she's in a heap of trouble.*

Their body language didn't seem to be sexual, but knowing Nate, that could change on a dime. The woman he was dressing down was likely going to end up handed off to Taz for punishment since he'd just joined the party. But as he watched, Kip became more curious about the little sub's identity when she kept tugging on what he was convinced was a wig. *Why are you hiding your hair, little sub?* In his experience, subs wore wigs to the club for one of two reasons. Either they were role playing or hiding. Since she hadn't actually been a part of tonight's production, he quickly ruled out role play.

Kip moved to the side hoping to get a look at the woman's face, but he was only catching fleeting glimpses. When he moved again, Kip didn't miss Nate Ledek's eyes flicker to him. The man's lips quirked but he didn't actually smile. *What the hell is going on?* Before he could step forward, Kip heard Nate ask, "Master Taz, would you like to play with this pretty little subbie?" When Taz smiled, Nate returned his attention to the woman he was now lifting off the bar. "Caila, go with Master Taz. Be honest with him about your limits or you'll be answering to me." *Caila? Caila Cooper? What the holy living fuck is she doing in a damned kink club?*

Taz led Caila away as Kip watched in stunned silence. He wasn't sure it was *his* Caila, but he damned well intended to find out. Realizing he'd just thought of her as his, sent his mind spinning completely out of control. *What the fuck?* She might not be his, but she damned well didn't belong in a sex club either. Pushing away from the wall, Kip found his path blocked by Master Nate, and the man was in full club owner mode.

"Where do you think you're going, Kip?"

Kip considered telling Nate to take a hike, but as the youngest of five boys, he'd learned a long time ago that arguing with authority figures rarely turned out well. "I'm interested in the woman Taz just left with. There is something familiar about her." *There. The truth without too much extra information.* Being the youngest sibling meant he'd acquired a wide variety of survival skills, including evasive answers.

Nate studied him for several seconds before nodding. "Be very careful how you handle this, Kip." For several seconds he considered asking Nate to explain his comment, but again, experience kicked in so Kip just nodded again. In a lot of ways, Nate reminded him his oldest brother, Sage. The only part of their personality that ran deeper than their sexual Dominance was their mind for business—and questioning Nate on this point would be challenging him on both levels. Drawing on experience, Kip knew there were a lot of ways *that* could play out—and none of them were good.

Moving through the small crowd, Kip searched the room for Taz, rather than the woman he'd escorted away, simply because he towered over almost everyone else in the room. He spotted Taz by one of the exits, but the little brunette wasn't with him. When he got close enough, he could tell from the conversation he could hear between the Dungeon Monitor and Nate that he was concerned about a security breach. Taz rubbed his hand over his face and turned to face Kip.

"I left my sweet, little charge sitting in the small alcove by the patio doors. I've got to take care of this." Kip could read the reluctance in Taz's expression—the man wasn't happy to put her in Kip's care and something about that annoyed the hell out of him. "I'm putting her in your care, Kip. Look out for her, Nate and I are both worried she'll make a decision she's going to regret. She isn't as experienced as she wants us to think she is, and that makes her a lone sheep in a room full of very experienced wolves." Kip knew his expression was probably reflecting his annoyance, but at this moment he didn't care. Without responding, Kip turned on his heel and made his way to the secluded area.

He heard a muffled gasp as he stepped into the small alcove and was surprised to find a Dom he didn't recognize standing over Caila Cooper. The man was clutching her wig in one hand as his other hand untangled the familiar long blonde waves of her real hair. She hadn't seen him enter the small space yet, but the Dom had. "There might be enough left of this little doll when I'm done, but I wouldn't count on it. Might as well find your own wench."

Caila's eyes darted to his and went wide with a look of pure relief before it was quickly replaced by embarrassment. He didn't want to shame her, but he damned well wasn't going to leave her here either. "What's her name?" Kip would bet his interest in the ranch the Dom hadn't even asked.

"Who the fuck cares. Look at her. I knew this was a wig, but it looks like it came from a thrift store. I'm taking her out back. I'll introduce her to my cat and then fuck her ass. Stick around and you can have her mouth." Kip didn't doubt the man intended to leave with her, but the rest of the garbage he'd spewed sounded like he'd been reading from a damned script.

Kip could see the tears gathering in Caila's eyes, damn it, *if she cries I'm going to kick his ass.* Caila's tears had always had a powerful effect on all the Morgan brothers. Even when they were kids and annoyed as hell with her; they all melted at the first sign of her tears. *Fuck me, she can be a real pain in the ass, but she damned well doesn't deserve this.*

"What do you say, little subbie? You sign up for being whipped by this Dom?" He wasn't going to give away the fact he knew her unless he had to, maybe she could salvage a little bit of dignity before he marched her happy ass out of there.

She shook her head vigorously before answering, "No, Sir." There was a small part of him that was impressed as hell she'd managed to keep it together enough to use proper protocol, but a much larger part was pissed as hell that she knew it.

"You heard the lady. You need to let her go."

"Fuck you. She hasn't said her safe word. She's just playing hard to get." Knowing the man intended to take Caila outside in the cold night air to whip her was enough to fuel Kip's nightmares for months. She was obviously terrified, and started shaking so hard Kip worried she was going to rattle apart. When she opened her mouth to speak, the man backhanded her. Kip was moving before the sound of the strike fell away. His fist connected with the man's jaw sending him staggering backward and pulling Caila along by her hair. The second punch dazed the jerk enough to release her, and Kip was grateful she'd had the good sense to run behind him.

CAILA WASN'T SURE whether to cheer or cry when Kip walked into the small alcove where Master Taz left her. She'd been shocked when the Dom holding her by her hair stepped into the small space once she'd been alone. Master Taz had assured her no one would bother her, so she'd assumed the patio doors were locked. *Remember what Pops always says about assuming?*

She'd tried to tell him she was waiting for Master Taz to return, but he hadn't seemed to care. Hell, she'd wondered if he even knew who Taz was because he hadn't acted like he recognized the man's name. He'd taken her by surprise when he yanked the wig from her head. She felt her hair fall against her back and saw him frown. Oddly enough, she understood his frustration with the unruly waves, they were the reason she favored ponytails and braids.

The man ripped the shirt she'd been wearing, exposing the bustier underneath and she saw his eyes widen. Well, well, looks like you've been holding out on me, captain." *Huh?* Before she could ask any questions, he started talking about how he planned to use her to get what he wanted as he hustled her to the door.

Seeing Kip Morgan step into the small alcove sent a strong wave of relief through her, and Caila stumbled before the man dragging her to the doors caught her. Noticing Kip, the jerk holding her seemed to falter for a split second before he started talking trash again. Caila wondered if the man had any good sense at all. *Do you have any idea who you are dealing with?* Kip Morgan might appear to be relaxed to someone who didn't know him well, but she wasn't one of the uninformed.

Kip wasn't a man you wanted to trifle with. Growing up in a house filled with boys, he'd learned at an early age to hold his own. She'd seen his strength and agility displayed many times over the years, his hard work on the ranch and their commercial grade home gym kept him in peak physical condition. When she saw the telltale twitch of the muscles around his jaw, a sure sign he was grinding his teeth together in frustration, she knew things were about to go over the edge. *Oh yeah, this is going nowhere fast.*

Once, when Brandt had been home on leave, he'd teased her about her latest disaster. "Don't worry, Calamity, it's just another SNAFU." When she'd questioned him about the acronym, he'd laughed as he explained, "Situation normal, all fucked up." He'd leaned down and tapped her on the nose. "See, my little Mistress of Mayhem, even the SEALs have a term for you." Even though she'd known he was teasing, his words had stung.

Another sharp pull of her hair by the jerk who'd yanked off her wig and torn her bustier made her stagger. The pain searing over her scalp was so sharp it blurred her vision for several seconds, and brought her attention back to her latest SNAFU. *Well, this sucks big green donkey dicks. I'm going to have to suck it up and admit Brandt was right.* The asshole holding her was yammering about going outside. She tuned him out, until Kip's question about being whipped shocked her back to awareness.

The thought of this man whipping her was terrifying. She felt her eyes fill with tears despite her best effort to hold them back. Caila had always known how each and every one of the Morgan brothers reacted to her tears, but she'd never exploited their reaction. Even as a kid, she had wanted their respect, not their pity.

Caila knew Kip considered her an annoyance, but she was convinced he wouldn't hesitate to make sure she was safe. Of course, right now that meant protecting her from the jerk manhandling her, not safe from him...and she didn't even want to think about the *chat* this situation was going to initiate. Yes, indeed...she'd tumbled into another mess head-first without even trying.

Fuck a three-legged duck, this time, my fall might not involve broken bones or stitches, but it's still going to be epic.

Chapter Ten

Aspen was floating on the cusp of blissful oblivion and basking in the warmth spreading over the surface of her skin as the relentless slap of the flogger heated her all the way to her core. The first strikes were so gentle she'd wondered if she'd imagined them, but they'd increased in intensity quickly, before Phoenix whispered, "Let's see how good your self-control is, sweet goddess. Do. Not. Come."

She learned quickly how much more powerful the sensations were when the intensity was random. The anticipation was all consuming, she was completely lost in the moment. The blindfold didn't keep her from knowing the difference between Mitch and Phoenix's touches. Mitch's was lighter...more about seduction, while Phoenix's was firmer. She suspected he was the stricter of the two.

She'd read everything she could get her hands on about the lifestyle as soon as she learned her friends were sexual Dominants. The collection of BDSM books, both fiction and non-fiction on her e-reader, would make the Library of Congress envious. After meeting Mitch Ames, she'd re-read most of the titles and by the time she'd discovered Phoenix Morgan was also a Dom she'd been able to identify the clues in his messages.

Mitch's dominance had been far more elusive when

they first met, and she might have missed the signs if she hadn't spent years dealing with Jax, Kyle, and Kent. Of course, having Doms as your best friends was a mixed blessing. It was particularly true when you were trying to earn respect among your Air Force peers and your friends were Special Forces legends with no shame when it came to micromanaging her.

Soft lips pressed against the sensitive skin below her ear. "If your mind is still *thinking* we aren't doing something right. I think it's time to step things up a bit." *How did he know I was thinking?* Aspen wasn't sure what Mitch's cryptic words meant until the cross she was bound to started to move. Tilting forward, Aspen gasped when she felt her center of balance shift. She was suddenly grateful for the extra straps they'd used. She wasn't sure what they had in mind until she felt cool lubricant drizzling down the crack of her ass.

Aspen felt her entire body tense as deft fingers slid over her rear entrance, rubbing the slick lube in circles over the tight ring of muscles. Gasping, she tried to move away from the intrusion, but her efforts were futile. "Is your mind still wandering, little sub?" When she didn't answer, a stinging swat landed on the tender crease at the top of her thighs.

Gasping for breath as the pain morphed into sexual need, Aspen finally managed to spit out the word no, but it wasn't enough. Another slap to the other side, this one harsher than the last, pulled her back to the moment. "No, Sir. My mind isn't wandering, Sir."

"That was much better, sweet goddess; your military training is going to serve you well in the play room." She was sure there was some sort of hidden message in Mitch's words, but her brain wasn't firing on all cylinders at the moment so she pushed the puzzle aside. For the first time she could remember, she allowed herself to completely surrender to the moment, letting the sensations flow over her without trying to justify her needs.

Aspen's release was building with each circle of Mitch's lubed finger around her rear entrance. The first press of his slick digit against the opening almost sent her over the edge. "Don't come, Athena, or we'll have to start all over." She hadn't heard Phoenix move, but his voice came from a spot directly in front of her. Straining to hear any clues helped refocus her thinking on her surroundings rather than the release she wasn't supposed to be chasing.

Mitch replaced one finger with two and continued stretching her. The burn faded quickly into a need so strong sweat beaded on her forehead. By the time, he slid a small plug into her, the combination of being tilted so far forward and her head spinning was making her so dizzy she worried she would be sick if they didn't remove the blindfold.

Aspen felt like her body had been high-jacked by nausea sweeping through her, the same thing had happened during one of her flight training exercises. Learning to fly by instruments alone required the pilot to fly with a hood over their head only allowing them to see the instrument panel, and it had almost been her undoing. Had it not been for a patient instructor who gave her more chances than he should have, she'd never have become a fighter pilot.

Voices swirled around her adding to her dizziness, and she felt herself start to gag as the cross was being raised and the blindfold pulled from her eyes. Years of training kicked in, and she moved her eyes to the other side of the room, it wasn't a perfect solution, but it was the closest thing she had to the horizon. Ryan Morgan stepped into her line of vision and she heard him say, "Don't move her and don't step in front of her. Let her eyes find a focal point, she'd doing exactly what she needs to do."

Embarrassment swept over her, but she didn't dare move her eyes until the room stopped spinning around the door she was focused on. *Fuck me, this is a new level of humiliation, even for me. What a way to screw up my own fantasy.*

PHOENIX HAD BEEN shocked when Ryan shouted, "Get the blindfold off her," as he jumped up onto the stage. Ryan had been a medic in the SEALs before resigning his commission to finish medical school. He'd recently taken over when Pine Creek's only physician retired. Ryan and Brandt had both recently married Joelle Phillips, who was hands down the smartest women Phoenix had ever met. He'd known Ryan his entire life, hell, they were cousins for Christ's sake, but he'd never seen Ry play the role of the physician in the club. The change in his persona was almost startling. Gone was the playful Dom who'd been focused on his wife's pleasure a few seconds earlier. In his place was a rock solid doctor who'd obviously seen, whatever Aspen was experiencing, before.

Mitch must have seen the same clues and seemed to understand Ryan's concern because he'd started tilting the St. Andrew's cross back up at the same time Phoenix pulled the soft silk fabric from Aspen's eyes. He'd been shocked to see the look of desperation in her expression, and *hell, is she green?* When she started swallowing convulsively, Ryan stepped further to the side cautioning them to stay out of her line of sight. The rest of his words were lost on Phoenix because as he focused on the beautiful woman in front of him.

He had no idea what had gone wrong, hell, he wasn't even sure *when* things had gone *off rails*, but at this point they were so far gone he couldn't even see the damned track. Brandt moved to his side, giving him a sympathetic look. Yep, being married had definitely been good for his older brother. The bitter man who'd returned from the SEALs had only started to fade when Brandt finally admitted his interest in Joelle. Every member of the Morgan family credited Joelle with the changes in the middle Morgan brother. She'd have had their undying devotion for that alone, but they loved her simply because of who she was.

Joelle was a world renowned chemist whose recent discovery launched cancer treatment decades into the future. Phoenix had a huge amount of respect for her and was relieved to realize she'd stepped up beside him. "She'll be okay. Vertigo isn't life threatening, and you know Master Ryan isn't going to take any chances with her safety."

Phoenix must have looked as confused as he felt because Brandt leaned around his sweet wife and said, "Vertigo often affects people when they are tilted at an odd angle, and they can't find any visual point of reference. That combined with anxiety—doesn't matter if it's just anticipation of pleasure, was enough to send her over the edge. She'll be fine, but I have to tell you, it's damned impressive to know she was a fighter pilot. Damned impressive, indeed."

He could only assume his brother was referring to how difficult it would have been to train to become instrument rated when she struggled with vertigo. Phoenix knew the "hood" pilots wore didn't completely cover their eyes, but it definitely prevented them from using visual orientation clues—something Aspen obviously needed. He'd seen Sage practice when he'd become instrument rated so he could fly the Morgan jet. Sage hadn't dealt with vertigo, but he'd still commented on how difficult it was to fly without any visual clues.

Phoenix wondered what motivated Aspen to pursue flying when it hadn't been something easily mastered. His best guess was her friendship with Jax and the Wests. According to her file, they'd been the ones to teach her to fly. Phoenix had been surprised to learn the former NFL player was the first to get his pilot's license—he'd be willing to bet Jax had been the only player on the team jet who was qualified to fly the damned thing.

"I don't know where your mind is, sweet brother of mine, but you need to refocus on Aspen. It looks like my other Master is satisfied she's going to be alright, and if she's anything like me she is going to be awfully embarrassed by all this." Joelle's hand swept in a wide arc indicating the crowd gathered around the stage.

Phoenix leaned over and pressed a soft kiss against her cheek. "I'm not sure I'll ever understand what you see in my knucklehead brother, but I'm proud to call you sister." He smiled when Brandt batted him upside the head. Damn, it was good to have his brother back. When Ryan turned to look in their direction, Phoenix stepped forward. Returning his attention to Aspen, he winked at her over his shoulder and said, "Make sure these two take good care of you, sweetheart. If they give you any trouble, you just let me know, and I'll rally the troops."

"Keep your lips off our woman and take care of your own, cousin." Ryan brushed past him, and Phoenix smiled when he saw Joelle's face light up when Ry pulled her into his arms. Moving in front of Aspen, Phoenix felt his heart clench at the look of devastation on her face. They'd wanted to play out a minor punishment scene, but they certainly hadn't intended for her to become ill.

Mitch stood behind Aspen, his arms circled protectively around her. God, she looked so young standing there wrapped in one of the club's soft subbie blankets. When her eyes met his, Phoenix watched them fill with unshed tears before she looked at the floor. Lifting her chin with his fingers, Phoenix shook his head. "Eyes on me, little sub. Why didn't you use your safe word?" The words came out harsher than he'd intended, but now that the adrenaline spike had passed, he was left with nothing but frustration. Damn, what if it had been something more serious? If she wasn't going to use her safe word, how would they know she was safe during a scene? Just thinking about hurting her terrified him.

He wrapped his large hand around the nape of her neck, and stroked the side of her chin with his thumb. The hesitance he saw in her eyes was going to haunt him. "We aren't angry. We know you aren't an experienced submissive, but it's important for us to walk you through this, so we don't end up in a similar unfortunate position next time."

"Next time? You'd play with me again? After I messed this up so bad?" The self-recrimination in her voice was as annoying as it was surprising. *How could a woman so beautiful and so brilliant be so fucking insecure?* Mitch looked at him over her shoulder with the same *what the fuck* expression Phoenix was sure mirrored his own.

"Let's take this discussion upstairs, shall we? But the answer to your question is, *absolutely*. This wasn't a *mess-*

up; it was a *lesson*—for all of us." Before they could lead her to the stairs, alarms started blaring. Doms who often helped out as dungeon monitors put their subs in the care of other Doms and sprinted toward the back of the club where a strobe light flashed. Phoenix knew there was an exit in that area, but the perimeter exits were only for emergency use unless they'd been opened for an outdoor event. Whoever had triggered the alarm was going to answer to Nate Ledek, and Phoenix didn't want to be anywhere close when that conversation took place.

KIP WAS CONVINCED his ears were going to start bleeding any minute. Holy shit, that alarm could wake the dead. The asshole who'd been manhandling Caila either hadn't read his membership contract or he didn't care, because he'd pushed through the doors and disappeared into the darkness. Kip had helped Phoenix install the system, so he knew the door locks re-set every five minutes when the club was open. When he'd asked Phoenix why his brother had grinned. "If someone hacks the door alarm to enter, they'll expect the system to still be disengaged if they try to escape. This assures us they won't be able to do that without drawing a whole lot of attention."

Watching Nate race out the door, Kip smiled to himself. *The prick who hit Caila deserves the ass-kicking Nate's going to give him.* Pulling Caila into his arms, Kip pressed her against his chest and covered her ear with his hand, there was no need for them both to go deaf. *Christ Almighty, turn that fucking thing off.*

Taz was only a second or two behind Nate, but he stopped long enough to ask for the guy's description and shut down the alarm before he also disappeared in the darkness. Kip slowly released his hold on Caila, but didn't let her step away. There wasn't a chance in hell either of them could hear anything over the ringing in their ears, so he didn't even try to ask her if she was alright. He brushed the pad of his thumb over her cheek to brush away the tracks her tears had left. He was careful not to put any unnecessary pressure on the deep red handprint marring her cheek. Seeing the evidence of the asshole's slap made Kip's vision go hazy with a red tint of rage.

"I'm sorry." He didn't hear the words, but he'd been able to read her lips. Shaking his head, Kip pulled her back into his arms, wondering why it felt like she was exactly where she belonged. Knowing Nate and Taz were going to want to interview her, he scooped her into his arms and making his way toward their office when he met Brandt.

"Calamity? Oh shit, please tell me she wasn't trying to break into the club." Ordinarily, Kip wouldn't have been annoyed by his brother's assumption, but tonight had turned out to be anything but ordinary.

"None of this is her fault. She was assaulted in the last alcove. She's damned lucky I got to her when I did. Grab her things, I'm taking her to Nate's office." Kip saw Brandt's eyebrows arch in surprise—so much for his reputation as the easygoing brother. Stalking past Brandt, Kip felt Caila's tears against his neck. "Don't cry, baby, he wasn't trying to hurt your feelings."

Hell, it was usually Kip who hurt her with his sharp words, but something changed the minute he realized who she was tonight. He wasn't sure why she was wearing a damned wig, but he intended to find out. *I'll find out, then walk away.* It sounded good when he repeated the words to himself, but for some reason, his heart and mind didn't seem to be on the same page.

Chapter Eleven

ASPEN HEARD THE alarm, but before she could ask what was going on, Phoenix picked her up and sprinted up a flight of stairs. She heard Mitch cursing as he ran around them, but she had no idea why. She watched from Phoenix's hold as they passed several ornate doors with large numbers carved in them. Aspen assumed they were the private rooms she'd read about on the club's website, but since she hadn't actually toured the club, she wasn't sure. The door Phoenix carried her through was already open. Obviously, Mitch had gotten it unlocked in record time.

When Phoenix set her on her feet, Aspen looked up and saw his eyes were practically shooting fire. His lips were pursed in a taut line that made him look furious. Her fight or flight instinct kicked in, and she took two quick steps backward before he wrapped his large hands around her upper arms and halted her retreat. "Where do you think you're going?" His barked question didn't do anything to ease her concern, and she cast a quick glance at the door. Could she make it before they caught her? Doubtful, but it might be her only option.

"Jesus, you're terrifying her. Let her go, for God's sake." Mitch's words had the desired effect, Phoenix released her immediately, his expression going from thunderous to confused.

"What? Why on Earth is she afraid of me? She should

be afraid of whatever was going on downstairs, not me. What the fuck?" Aspen felt some of the tension drain away at his confusion, but she didn't make any effort to close the distance between them.

Mitch moved so he was standing in front of her. "Little goddess, Master Phoenix was worried about your safety, which explains our record-setting dash up the stairs. He isn't angry with you, just the situation. The last part of our well-planned evening of seduction has been a cluster fuck, to say the least." When she didn't say anything, he simply smiled. "Feeling a little overwhelmed?" This time she nodded, and he chuckled.

Shaking his head, Mitch's expression changed before her very eyes. "I have to tell you, I'm damned impressed you managed to make it through flight school with vertigo, but I'm pissed as hell that you didn't use your safe word. This is the only warning you're going to get, darlin'—make that mistake again and we won't let you come for a week."

"And we'll make sure it's the longest week of your life because we'll play with you morning, noon, and fucking night." Phoenix had finally recovered enough to join their conversation, but his frustration was still simmering just below the surface. Aspen knew for a man whose entire life revolved around being exacting and precise, this evening was a disaster of Biblical proportions.

"But we won't let you come. Don't be fooled, *mon cher*, it will be a punishment far worse than any spanking." Mitch's sly smile told her all she needed to know. All of her thoughts about how nice it would be to have them playing with her again evaporated into thin air. Remembering one of the lessons she struggled with most when she joined the Air Force, Aspen held back the comment tap dancing on the tip of her tongue. *No need to throw gas on the fire.* Mitch tapped his finger against the end of her nose and smiled. "Wise decision, Captain."

MITCH WATCHED THE fire dance in her eyes and fought back a smile at the almost imperceptible upward tilt of her chin—*that's it, baby, I love a challenge.* "We're going to play with you before we go back downstairs and find out what all the ruckus was about. But before we start, let's make sure we've gotten all the drab, but necessary *first time together* discussion out of the way." Mitch nodded to Phoenix to let his friend know he could begin. He'd learned early in their friendship, Phoenix was more interested in the rules and protocol of BDSM than Mitch was, so it seemed natural to let him take the lead.

"We'll use the club's stop light system since you aren't an experienced player and we won't want you to risk being confused then it matters the most. It is the one you seemed familiar with downstairs, it's also the system we'll use in our playroom at the ranch." When she raised a brow in surprise, Phoenix shook his head. "We'll talk more about that later. For tonight, you will be allowed to ask questions as long as you are respectful and it's pertinent to what is happening in this room."

Mitch stepped forward, intent on getting through this before the club's closing time. *Christ, if I leave this to Phoenix, he'll be whipping out spreadsheets and cutting the lights for a fucking PowerPoint presentation.* "We've read your application and studied your limit list."

"Yeah, what there was of it. What the hell were you thinking leaving some of that stuff on there? Knife play? Really?"

When she started to open her mouth, Mitch pressed two fingers against her lush lips. "Master Phoenix was more upset about that point than I was. I feel as though you are too inexperienced to have made informed decisions, but, I also understand his concern. Walking out into the club without a limit list for protection is tantamount to being dipped in blood and dropped in a shark tank. The sadists and extreme players would spot you in a heartbeat."

"And eat you alive—and not it a good way. Fuck, I don't even want to think about what could have happened if you'd pulled that stunt in another club." Phoenix had gone ape shit when he'd see Aspen's list, despite Nate's assurance it wasn't uncommon for inexperienced subs to be completely clueless. The former SEAL had grinned before explaining how effective club tours were for adding to their lists.

Mitch wasn't thrilled with her list either, he'd have thought her exposure to so many Doms would have given her some insight. Nate had shaken his head and disagreed. "She knows plenty of Alpha males and sexual Dominants, but she had never known one *intimately*. And all of her association with Doms has been as friends, so she has no experience seeing them as anything other than overprotective and bossy. Perhaps if she was friends with other submissives, she might have an opportunity to gain a better understanding of the dynamics of the lifestyle."

It was true, Cameron Barnes was one of the strictest Masters in the lifestyle, and he treated Aspen like a princess because she'd saved Cecelia's life. Jax, Kent, and Kyle had all known her since they were young and treated her like a little sister. Aspen's heart knew what her body needed, but her mind was going to fight them until they could prove their mettle.

He and Phoenix agreed their best option was to associate every point of Dominance they won with an equal or greater point of pleasure. He hated to make the comparison to Pavlov's classical conditioning, but it was simply a fact of nature. Our minds make associations between actions and pleasure. They needed to cement that association in her mind—and they needed to do it quickly. A woman as smart as Aspen wouldn't spend a lot of time chasing what she was looking for only to settle for anything less than amazing.

Mitch shot a glare at Phoenix that would be damned hard to misinterpret. He wasn't about to let his friend blow this simply because he was annoyed about a damned limit list. One of the things Mitch had learned over the years was often it was the most intelligent people who could be totally derailed by something inconsequential. He preferred to choose his battles carefully.

Pulling her hands into his, Mitch smiled. "Let's agree that your list is incomplete, and for now we'll play well within bounds of what Master Phoenix and I deem appropriate and safe for you. You already know your friends have given us their stamp of approval, and you know we'll never hurt you—well, at least not in a way that doesn't lead to pleasure." Her eyes darkened as the pupils dilated and her shoulders lost some of their tension when he winked at her. God, she was adorable when she was off-kilter.

Phoenix finished reviewing the stop light system and added, "I'm not sure I can overemphasize how important safe words are. They protect you, and they assure us you won't let things go so far you become frightened or injured. Remember, this lifestyle is about our *mutual* pleasure."

"Once we know you better—what you like and don't like, what brings you pleasure and what doesn't, we'll expect to hear the word yellow a lot less frequently." Mitch wanted her to know neither of them was looking at this evening as a one-time encounter, but he wasn't sure she'd heard that part of the message. *Not to worry, little sub. We'll tell you as many times as it takes.*

ASPEN TRIED TO control her responses to Mitch and Phoenix, but none of the biofeedback tricks she'd learned as a pilot worked. Her mind knew the consequences of her accelerated heart rate and respiration, but her body wouldn't listen to reason. Her nipples drew into points so tight she could feel the throb of each beat of her heart as it echoed in each one. Squeezing her thighs together in an effort to relieve the need building in her sex, her face flushing at the knowing looks on their faces.

"Feeling needy, little sub?" Mitch's teasing words set off mixed emotions. She desperately wanted them to touch her—God in heaven, she needed to come. But on the other hand, she knew everything she'd ever thought she knew about sex was about to be shattered into a million pieces, and there was something unsettling about that humbling realization. How could she be so attracted to two men? For the first time since she'd decided to join Mountain Mastery, Aspen was beginning to think she was in over her head.

Phoenix's sure fingers gripped her chin and tilted her face up to his. "You're getting lost in your own head, pet. It's time for us to push that bothersome distraction out of your mind. You've lead us on a merry chase for months, I'm going to show you what becomes of sweet little subs who try to hide from their Masters. Since you didn't technically belong to us, this punishment is going to be as much about satisfying our needs as it is about correcting a behavior we don't believe is in your best interest."

Aspen didn't understand what he meant and said so. Mitch surprised her by reminding her about the contract she'd signed when she joined the club. "Did you read the contract you signed, *cher*?" She wasn't born yesterday, and she damned well recognized a lose-lose question when she heard one. *Like I'm going to answer a question that falls directly in line with...do you still beat your wife?* When she didn't answer, he raised a brow in question. "Do you really want to start this way, sweetness? Both Master Phoenix and I are prepared to meet your challenges."

"Oh, indeed we are. This is a *begin as you intend to go* moment, baby. Think carefully about how you want the next few minutes to go for you because I have to tell you, I'm dying to introduce my palm to your bare ass." Her breath hitched, and Aspen felt an unexpected rush of arousal dampen her sex. *Holy shitacky.* "What did you say?" *Say? I didn't say anything.*

Mitch broke the silence, laughing out loud. "Babe, you have to let that lingo go. I'm going to catch it and set your ass on fire every time I hear it." Turning his attention to Phoenix he explained. "It's a slang term for being extremely frustrated or confused. And her use of the word reminds me how young she is. In general, I'm not a huge fan of slang and believe me, growing up in the south, I could bury you in it. And in this particular instance, I have the feeling she wasn't planning to say it out loud. Now, while it was a great attempt at distraction, little goddess, back to Master Phoenix's original question. Did you read the contract you signed? Specifically, did you read the section that stated you would put yourself in the hands of the Dom or Doms Master Nate tasked with your training?"

Since the questions were more specific and less open to misinterpretation, Aspen was more willing to answer—and she did. *I'm less likely to fuck up if the questions are clear...hopefully.* "Well, a large part of putting yourself in our hands involves trusting us to give you what you need, even when it conflicts with what you want or what *you* think you need."

Phoenix chuckled. "I can tell you from watching my brothers and their wives, there will be plenty of opportunities for discussion about this because we are always going to err on the side of the angels when it comes to you."

"I've been taking care of myself for a long time and..."

"And we found you despite your best efforts to elude us." Phoenix had a valid point, and she knew it, but she wasn't going down without a fight.

"But..." She made a gesture indicating she was talking about them both, "you guys have resources most people can only dream of. And I know Micah helped as well, so I don't think this is a fair comparison." Even she could hear the defiance in her voice, and she was sure they hadn't missed it.

"Captain, that's the lamest thing I think I've ever heard you say." Aspen noticed Mitch slipped back into the military mindset whenever he felt she was out of line. She knew he still took missions with the Wests' team, but she suddenly realized she didn't know what he did the rest of the time. She knew his family had various business holdings, but from what she'd read he had only a minimal interest. Yet, he didn't seem like the type to sit around all day watching soap operas either...*interesting.*

Vowing to do more research as soon as she got back to

her hotel room, she looked up at Mitch and smiled, knowing he'd see right through the gesture. She'd been so focused on Mitch, Aspen missed Phoenix shifting his position. He pulled her sideways until she was pressed against his chest. "Enough chatting. Let's get started. Remember, use your safe words if you need them."

She had no idea how he moved so quickly, but before she realized she'd been moved, she was laying across his knees. Her bare ass was peaked in a way that left her toes bouncing in the air and the tips of her fingers barely brushing the floor. Wrapping her hands around his ankle, she tried to steady the rocking motion before she ended up dizzy from the quick up-ending.

"Your safety is our priority. A good Dom cherishes and protects his submissive. And, honors the gift of her trust." The first slap on her bare flesh made her gasp. It hadn't been particularly harsh, but it had taken her by surprise. She was more prepared for the next blow but heard herself squeak anyway. Damn, her ass felt like it was on fire and she'd bet he wasn't anywhere near finished. Aspen felt herself sliding slowly down a slope of desire until she settled in a daze where the pain slowly shifted to something altogether different. The heat from the swats was becoming a burning desire she didn't understand. Why wasn't she screaming her safe word? And for the love of God, why was she so wet that she could feel it soaking the folds of her sex?

Chapter Twelve

PHOENIX COULD PRACTICALLY hear the wheels in Aspen's mind spinning as she tried to rationalize her body's reaction to the pain. When he landed the last swat, he leaned down to press his lips against the hot pink skin of her rounded ass cheek. "Your skin turns the most delectable shade of pink; it's the color of the heart of a summer sweet sun-ripened melon." Pressing another kiss to the baby soft flesh, he felt his cock harden and knew she would be able to feel the evidence of her effect on him before long. "Hell, I may spank you just for the sheer joy of seeing this color again."

Phoenix slid his fingers between her legs, leisurely stroking the soft folds of her sex but not pushing between the swollen lips. Her honey coated his fingers, and he wanted to slide them between his lips and taste her. "It seems your body has an intimate understanding of the link between pleasure and pain, even if your mind is struggling to make sense of it." He stroked the outer lips of her pussy and smiled when she moaned. Watching Aspen's back arch as she tried to press the sensitive tissues against his fingers was one of the sexiest things he'd ever seen.

He'd played with submissives for years and had rarely walked away feeling anything other than sexual satisfaction. Phoenix always made sure the subs he played with were sated even though there was no personal connection between them. But there was something different this time, and he wasn't entirely sure he could even describe it. The only thing he knew for certain was he'd enjoyed watching the imprint of his hand blossom with color on her delicious ass. He'd reveled in the feel of her satiny skin beneath his calloused palm, it humbled him to hear how quickly her whimpers of discomfort had subtly transformed into the sweet moans of desire. Christ, those delicious sounds were going to echo in his mind forever.

"We'll give you what you want, sweet Athena, but you'll have to be patient. Aside from our combined limit lists, there is only one thing off the table as far as your pleasure is concerned. We'll never compromise your safety, nor will we stand by and allow you to put yourself in jeopardy." He continued to tease her slick folds with the tips of his fingers, smiling at Mitch when she growled in frustration.

"What Master Phoenix is trying to impress upon you, Aspen is how seriously we take protecting what we consider ours." Phoenix felt her stiffen ever so slightly at Mitch's words. He thought she might be planning to protest their claim, but a quick flick of his finger against her clit pushed any dissenting thoughts she'd had right out of her head. Damn, he loved the way her body shuddered under his touch. "Now, up you go."

He'd planned to stand her up slowly, but she'd bounced to her feet the second he'd spoken. When she swayed, Mitch clasped his hands around her waist, steadying her. "Next time, wait for one of us to help you. There are physical aspects of the lifestyle you'll learn over time, but for now, put yourself in our hands." When she frowned at him, Mitch shook his head. "Frowning at your Dom is never a good idea, *mon cher*. Consider this your only warning. The next time one of us is on the receiving end of that look, you'll find yourself unable to sit comfortably for a few days."

Aspen wasn't sure who she was the most frustrated with…Mitch for his high-handed declaration or herself for not calling him out. She intentionally blanked her expression and watched him closely. The goal was to give the appearance of compliance while holding her "fuck you" attitude firmly in place. She'd learned at an early age how to use both skills to her advantage…the vacant look had saved her ass more times than she could count. And using her internal defiance as a shield had often been the only way she knew to avoid being hurt by others' opinions.

Mitch studied her for so long she started to fidget despite her determination to remain still. The corner of his mouth quirked up, and she knew he was trying to hold back his smile. He was toying with her. She knew it, but it was still working…*dammit*.

"You know, little goddess, I think you are far more complicated than Master Phoenix, or I anticipated." She tilted her chin up fractionally, enough to be noticed by someone paying attention, but not enough to be blatantly disrespectful. "I had assumed the attitude was abeyant military training you hadn't yet shaken—but, now I don't think that's the case. I think it's smoke and mirrors. You hide behind it, even if it's internalized." *Shit! I'm not getting into this with him…them.* Hoping he wouldn't sense how close he was to the truth, she didn't respond. *Well, if this isn't the shit frosting on my crappy cupcake of a day.*

MITCH WANTED TO laugh out loud—*damn it, I hope like hell she knows how to play poker. Sweet baby Jesus, we'll have her naked in three hands at the club's next casino night. Fucking perfect.* He loved the way her eyes broadcast everything she was thinking, even when she tried valiantly to hide behind her glower. When she was intrigued, her eyes were impossibly wide. Arousal caused her pupils to dilate so much they only left a narrow ring of green remaining. And the flash of fire as the color faded to ice green when she was angry was so captivating he wondered how often he would annoy her intentionally simply to see her reaction. This blank look was straight up pissing him off. But it was the deep jade of arousal he knew would be the most addicting.

"Aspen, don't think for a minute I don't see through this façade. Any attempt to hold back your response will be seen as a personal challenge, *cher.*"

"You'll deny yourself a lot of pleasure with that nonsense, sweetness." Mitch watched Phoenix trail his fingers over the heated flesh of her ass before cupping the round globe in his heated palm. Her gasp made Phoenix grin down at her. "Still tender from your spanking, little goddess?" Mitch knew his friend had planned to give her several stripes with his belt, but her mental step back must have warned him it would only serve to push her further into herself.

They knew it took time to develop a level of trust that allows submissives total surrender, and they'd barely scratched the surface with Aspen—but it didn't mean he wasn't anxious to know she was giving them everything.

When they'd had a chance to build a solid foundation of trust, it would provide a springboard for everything good the lifestyle had to offer. Then—and only then would they'd be able to use punishment to break through any attempt she made to stonewall. For now, he and Phoenix needed to keep her off-balance every chance they had, it was the only way he knew to give her a chance to get out of her own head.

"*Cher*, all that thinking is going to cause you nothing but trouble when we're in a scene."

"And let me assure you, my sweet Athena—we are most definitely in a scene." Mitch was relieved to see Phoenix had lightened his approach. He didn't want his friend's intensity overwhelming Aspen before they had a chance to show her how amazing single-minded focus could be when it was directed toward her pleasure.

"I understand all this in theory, but it's a lot harder to shut down my head than I thought it was going to be. Damn, I studied this...I should be able to do it, right? I'm just supposed to do what you tell me. How hard can that be? After all, I was in the Air Force...I know how to take orders. Not that I ever was really good at blindly following along if I didn't see the point, but still, I know how this is done." Mitch didn't even try to hold back his laughter. Hell, he had no idea how she'd managed all that without a single breath.

"While I appreciate your stream of conscious rambling because it's damned enlightening—for now, I don't want to hear you say another word unless it's one of your safe words." When she nodded, he pressed his lips to hers. What was supposed to be a chaste kiss to calm her, turned into a firestorm the instant his lips touched hers. Every single cell in his body felt as if it had suddenly been electrified. All his best intentions were pushed to the back of his mind, and the only thing he could think about was sinking his cock so deep in her he'd be able to feel her heartbeat.

Mitch had never come so close to completely losing control with a woman, let alone with a submissive during a scene. He and Phoenix had scripted this evening to the point he'd worried there wouldn't be a spontaneous moment left—hell, even Aspen's near meltdown hadn't derailed him as much as this kiss. Nothing mattered but this moment and the woman now crushed against his chest. He plundered her mouth with his, using his tongue to search every corner, every small niche before swallowing her soft sigh. He cataloged everything, every whimper, and moan—committing to memory exactly what he'd done to elicit the response. Each whisper of sound was another step in her surrender and Mitch relished it for what it was—a sweet gift of trust.

Chapter Thirteen

Aspen tried to keep her head in the game, but holy hell, Mitch Ames could kiss. His lips were hot and silky soft, and when he'd slammed his mouth over hers everything around her faded. The intensity would have frightened her if she hadn't seen the soft look in his eyes a split second before he robbed her of all cognitive function. *Somebody should probably alert EMS because I'm not sure I'll remember how to breathe on my own after this.* When he finally pulled back, she sucked in a deep breath hoping her eyes would be able to focus again.

"Damn, I love seeing that dazed look. Master Phoenix, I think we might have just found the first key to helping our lovely sub get out of her own head."

"Let's test your hypothesis." Before she could shift her fuzzy focus to the second man standing in front of her, he pulled her into his arms, hugging her so tightly she was conscious of every breath she fought to pull in. She felt as if she'd been bound by his arms and the effect it had on her body was startling. Trying to sort it out in her mind, the only thing she could think of was she'd that needed the reassurance he still wanted her after the punishment he'd given her.

Phoenix pulled back and slid the calloused pads of his fingers along the edge of her chin. "What are you thinking about?" She blinked up at him trying to decide how truthful she should be when he frowned. "Don't edit. I know that look. You are trying to figure out how to phrase it, and baby you'd only do that for one of two reasons. One, you don't think we can handle the truth, or two, you want to hide who you really are from us."

"So which is it, *cher*?" Aspen knew she was well and truly in over her head. They were so much more experienced, and she'd never considered how dramatically it would tip the scales in their favor.

"I...well, I was wondering... God, this is so embarrassing."

She'd barely gotten the words out when both men shook their heads. Phoenix wrapped his large hands around her wrists and leaned forward ever so slightly. "Let's see if I can help you. You're confused by the rush of heat you felt when you were bound by my arms."

Mitch's grin was far too knowing for her comfort. "*Cher*, your pulse just kicked up, and there isn't a Dom worth his salt who would have missed that hitch in your breathing at Master Phoenix's words. Don't ever be embarrassed by your body's response to kink."

"God, no. Relish it because we're fucking thrilled to know bondage is something we're going to be able to explore together. Fuck, it makes me hard just thinking about how sweet you'll look bound with soft jute rope or silk scarves."

"Jesus, Joseph, and sweet Mother Mary, there's a visual to give a man a killer hard-on. Damn." In her peripheral vision, Aspen saw Mitch shift and reposition the impressive erection outlined by his soft leather pants. She heard both men groan. "You'd better stop looking at my junk, baby, or this is going to be over long before any of us are ready for it to end."

She bit her tongue to keep from begging him to prove it. Aspen didn't know a lot about their lifestyle or dealing with Doms during scenes, but she knew enough about Alpha men, in general, to know they didn't usually respond well to being *pushed*. She'd been friends with Kent, Kyle, and Jax for a long time; and the one thing she'd learned was the best way to get them to do something *her* way was to convince them it was *their* idea. But since none of them had ever complicated their friendship with sex, so she doubted her wily ways would work with the two delicious men standing in front of her. *Probably should have considered this a little sooner, Asp.* Damn and double damn...sometimes she really hated that pesky little inner voice. Shooing the devilish diva from her thoughts, Aspen tried to refocus on the men stealing her sanity.

PHOENIX WAS THRILLED to see the look of hunger in Aspen's eyes. And he recognized the signs of a woman who spent far too much time alone. Her whispered self-talk was just this side of inaudible and he hadn't caught it all, but he'd heard enough to know she recognized dealing with the two of them would be different from her friendship with the Wests and Jax McDonald. *And right she is.*

"Come here. I want to taste you. The look on Master Mitch's face makes me want to have a sample of my own. And this time, I want you to stop trying to figure it out and simply enjoy it." He'd stepped back earlier and now, rather than yanking her into his hold, Phoenix waited for her to take the two steps needed to close the gap between them.

Mitch teased him about being too rules driven with subs, but he was fairly sure that wasn't going to be the case with Aspen. As his lips sealed over hers, Phoenix knew this woman was his future, and damn it looked an awful lot like Brandt's life. He and Brandt were the closest of the Morgan brothers in age and had always been opposites in almost every way. The only thing they'd always agreed on was their mutual respect for protocol—Brandt's version had been the military, Phoenix applied his to the rules of programming.

Before his mind could process the rest of the track it had been on, Aspen's response to his kiss obliterated every rational thought from his head. He'd never met a woman who responded as quickly and with as much fire. She'd done the same thing downstairs on stage. She hadn't even been able to see their faces, but her body had definitely recognized them.

Sage had once told him Coral didn't fully submit unless he was touching her. At the time, Phoenix had chalked his oldest brother's comment up to *love blindness*, but now he was beginning to understand. When he slid his warm palm up her spine, Aspen moaned into their kiss and the erotic sound vibrated all the way to his cock. She arched into him, her taut stomach pressing against his erection. *Yeah, there's no chance in hell she doesn't know the effect she is having on me.*

It wasn't easy keeping the kiss in check—hell, any lapse in his usual iron-clad control would have him pushing her up against the door and sinking in without a thought to the consequences. He needed to take a step back and make sure she understood exactly what they had in mind. Aspen's soft moan when she realized he was ending the kiss gave him hope she still wanted the two of them. He hadn't enjoyed the punishment scene, but it had cleared the air between them.

Once her eyes cleared, Phoenix smiled at her. The only

thing more satisfying to a Dom than waiting for the fog of lust to lift from their submissive's eyes was hearing them screaming their Dom's name when they came apart. He was planning to enjoy both before this evening was finished. "I love seeing your sparkling green eyes try to focus after I kiss you. It's how I know I've done it right."

"I think both of you know exactly what effect you have on the women you play with." Phoenix frowned when she turned toward Mitch, and he noticed his friend's expression mirrored his own.

"Want to explain exactly what you mean by that comment, *cher*? I'm working hard to hold my response in check until I'm certain I've interpreted it correctly."

Aspen's focused shifted between them several times and Phoenix almost laughed as her facial expressions spelled out everything she was thinking. She'd gone from confused by the question, to puzzled by their expressions, to resigned she was alone in a room with two men who were—in her view, clueless. He might not have any sisters, but there wasn't a Dom in the world who hadn't seen that *you are dumb as a rock* look on a sub's face.

Phoenix had been called a lot of things, but dumb wasn't one of them. The only person who'd ever come close was his mom when she'd felt he'd ignored some point of etiquette. It was usually something he thought was insignificant or obscure, but his mom considered egregious. Yeah, he'd definitely seen this look before.

Aspen's voice brought him back to the moment, and he hated to see the concern in her eyes. "Did you think I was being disrespectful? Because I can assure that isn't the case. I just assumed you already knew how devastating your kisses are. You don't kiss exactly the same, but I think that only enhances the effect, geez Louise. How did you not know this? You're an academic for crying out loud. What were you? Like seven or eight when you qualified for Mensa, and Einstein over there..." She gestured to Mitch, who was now grinning from ear-to-ear, "his I.Q. tops most nuclear engineers. So I'm totally not buying the, *we didn't know we could melt a woman from the inside out* routine."

Phoenix wanted to laugh out loud. Hell, his mother was going to love this woman—talk about being cut from the same cloth. Something inside him clicked as the last of his reservations faded away. He fought to hold back his smile and knew he'd failed when he saw relief move over her face. Her lips twitched, and her slender shoulders relaxed as she realized they were actually pleased with her assessment of their kisses.

Mitch stepped forward and pulled her close. "I'm glad you cleared that up, darlin', and it's easy to see you've done your homework."

"I had to do the background on Phoenix, and it wasn't difficult because he didn't have any clearance ratings yet. But you? Oh, you were much more challenging, as I'm sure you already know. But I did manage to find out a few things, Mitchell Markham Ames...nice monogram, by the way."

Phoenix didn't even try to hold back his laughter. Mitch shook his head, his scowl nothing even close to intimidating. *"Cher*, you've just earned yourself a bigger plug for blabbing that little tidbit."

For the first time, Aspen blushed, but she seemed to recover quickly. "Okay, but just so you know...it was worth it to see Master Phoenix smile." *What?* Hearing her call him Master Phoenix sent an inordinate amount of blood rushing to his cock, but he made a note to talk to her about the fact she didn't think he smiled enough. *Hell, she's probably right. It's not like this is the first time I've heard it. Fuck, yet another thing she and my mom agree on.*

Mitch backed her toward the bed and Phoenix watched as her pupils dilated and her breathing became little more than soft panting. Jesus, if she was already reacting this intensely, what's she going to be like when they were both inside her hot little body, their focus solely on her pleasure? He hoped like hell they all survived it.

ASPEN WAS GASPING for breath and so wet she could feel the first trickles of moisture wetting her inner thighs. When she reached to wipe it away, Phoenix shackled her wrist with his large hand. "Don't. It's very satisfying to know we've had such a profound effect on you. Not only do your orgasms now belong to us, this sweet syrup is also ours to enjoy." It was a good thing he'd helped her up onto the bed because her knees had almost folded out from under her.

In a rare moment of openness during their on-line chat, Phoenix had revealed he'd never felt as *smooth* with women as his brothers. She was overwhelmed by the words he'd just spoken. She wondered why he didn't feel he measured up to his brothers. In her opinion, both men were handling the evening remarkably well...and taking into account her earlier meltdown, it was saying a lot.

Their hands moved over her body in torturously slow movements, and her desire ramped up with every passing second. Each time she closed her eyes, they stopped until she once again lifted the lids and focused on one of them. "We want you to know who's making your body sing. There will definitely be times we'll want to blindfold you. Taking away one sense heightens the others, but tonight we want to be able to see you."

"There is a lot of truth to the old adage about the eyes being the windows to the soul, *cher*," Mitch spoke from the side, and she had been so focused on Phoenix she hadn't even seen him move. "It will help us learn what gives you pleasure versus those touches you don't enjoy. Since we haven't played together before, we need to learn all we can about your lovely body. In time, we'll know every inch…"

"We'll know your body better than you do in no time," Phoenix interjected.

"But for now, we'll all learn together. What's your safe word, *cher*?" Both men waited patiently why she repeated what they told her about the stop light system. "And where are we now, sweetness?"

"Green…really, really green. So green I'm going to be mistaken for a tree or a frog or a fucking tractor if you don't get on with it." She heard their chuckles, but it didn't speed them up any. Phoenix's fingers were sliding slowly through her wet folds but never pausing where she needed his touch most. Lifting her hips didn't help, he simply tsked at her efforts.

"Don't worry, baby, we're going to take you there, just let go. Put yourself in our hands." When she sighed and forced herself to relax, he surprised her by pressing two fingers into her channel, the sudden invasion set off a firestorm in her sex. She was completely unprepared for the orgasm that thundered its way to the surface. Her core contracted, and it felt like electrical pulses raced up her spine. "Fuck, baby, your vaginal muscles are squeezing my fingers so tight. I can't wait to feel them milking my cock."

Aspen's entire body was shaking so hard from the aftereffects of her release her teeth rattled together. She gasped, trying to pull oxygen into her lungs and hold back the powerful emotions threatening to steamroll her. Having experienced adrenaline drop firsthand, she recognized the signs and knew she needed to ride out the storm. *Holy shit, if you can't handle something this lightweight, you'll never be able to cut it as a submissive.* She'd just experienced the most intense orgasm of her life, without any consideration to their satisfaction.

"Master Phoenix, I believe we're going to have to keep our sub either very engaged or totally exhausted so she doesn't worry herself into a *fit of hysteria* as my granny used to say."

"Where did you go, sweet Athena?" She wasn't fooled by Phoenix's soft tone, she damned well recognized an order no matter how sweet it was given.

"I was wondering about you…well, I mean, about your… Geez, this is so embarrassing." Neither of them said a word, simply watched her. Damn, she hated the awkward silence, but she knew from dealing with her friends, Doms were very patient—silent and predatory when they wanted information. Hell, she'd tried to outlast Kyle West one time, and she'd learned just how uncomfortable silence could be. He'd shown up unannounced at her college dorm one evening, taken her to dinner and proceeded to interrogate her about a guy he'd heard she was dating. A few questions and the brooding silence. *Longest dinner of my life.* She still didn't know how the story made it all the way to Coronado.

"Unbelievable. I swear she goes on mental road trips without even saying goodbye. It gives me an appreciation for Kent and Kyle's complaints about Tobi." Aspen loved Tobi, so at the mention of her friend's name, she shot Mitch a scathing look. "Be careful, *cher*. I wasn't trying to disrespect your friend, but we both know she checks in and out with remarkable ease." Aspen nodded, reluctantly conceding the point.

She took a deep breath as she tried to get up the nerve to address her concerns and her face was already flushed. Cursing her fair complexion, she decided to just blurt it out. After everything she'd done, there was no reason for her to be intimidated about a simple conversation about sex. "You didn't come. Neither of you got to come. I did…boy, did I ever. But it doesn't seem fair. And why would you want to stick around if you aren't getting anything out of the deal? Damn, I don't know what I was thinking coming here. And two men? Like I have a prayer of keeping two men happy, hell, the only boyfriend I ever had dumped me because I mentioned needing…" Shit! What on Earth was she doing telling them about her one and only boyfriend?

Cripes, like it wasn't humiliating enough having Kent know about it? He'd heard the guy bitching about her in some damned bar in Germany. Only she could get dumped on one continent and ratted out on another. From what she'd heard, the fight hadn't lasted long, but it had cost Kent a night in his CO's office listening to his commander rail on about how SEALs didn't come out of barroom brawls with black eyes. The man hadn't been mad Kent punched her ex in the mouth, but he'd been seven kinds of pissed because the guy had given Kent a shiner. *Typical.*

Chapter Fourteen

MITCH HAD HEARD the story not long after it happened, but it hadn't been until he'd met Aspen that he'd known whose honor Kent had been defending. After meeting her, Mitch had questioned Kent about Aspen's ex. The story was one he'd heard dozens of times. A submissive isn't getting what she needs out of his or her sex life, asks their partner for *more*, even though they don't usually even know what it is they're looking for. The partner takes it as an affront to their sexual prowess, and there were several versions of the outcome, and none of them were ever pleasant.

He'd been pleased to hear Kent kicked the guy's ass, but now he saw the damage the asshat's words had done, Mitch wanted his own shot at him. He'd already told Phoenix the story, so they'd been prepared for this to come up at some point. But he had to admit, he hadn't expected it to be an issue so soon. Smiling at her, Mitch said, "Someday, we're going to have a conversation about your ex, but not tonight."

"You didn't think we were finished, did you?" Phoenix's question seemed to surprise her. And if her puzzled expression was any indication, Aspen had assumed they'd walk away from her. *Oh yeah, her ex definitely has another beating coming.* Phoenix pulled her closer but didn't completely close the distance between them. Keeping his hands wrapped around her shoulders, Mitch watched as he leaned down until they were practically nose to nose before he spoke again. "I can assure you, we are most definitely not finished with you, little goddess. I, for one, can hardly wait to push into your sweet heat. The fact you've already come once is as it should be."

All the time he'd been talking, Phoenix had been backing her slowly to the edge of the bed. It was time for them to show her exactly what they had planned. Phoenix lifted her easily onto the bed, then took the condom Mitch handed him. "Where are we, sweet goddess? Give me a color." Phoenix asked the question while sheathing himself, all without ever taking his eyes from hers.

Mitch was relieved to hear her soft response, assuring them she was *totally green*. Sweet words to any Dom's ears. He positioned himself near her upper torso, pressing his lips against hers before kissing his way to her ear. "Master Phoenix is going to fuck your sweet pussy while I enjoy your mouth, *cher*. I'll give you all the warning I can, and if you don't want to swallow you'll need to stop at my first warning." He always tried to give subs the option, it was after all their choice.

"I'll consider it a gift." Those five simple words stole his breath, and he knew in that moment he'd never be able to let her go. Leaning back so he could watch Phoenix claim her sweet pussy, Mitch was shocked at how much he enjoyed watching the two of them come together for the first time. The soft sounds she made as Phoenix pushed forward fractionally in a slow thrust and retreat went straight to his cock.

"Fucking hell, your pussy is so tight and hot. You're burning me alive, sweetheart." Phoenix looked at Mitch. "If you don't want to miss out, you'd better jump in, because our lovely sub is about to shred my control with those sweet sounds she's making. Her pussy muscles are already quaking. Christ in heaven, you're killing me, sweetheart.

Mitch wasn't about to be left out of the fun, stripping in under a minute, he palmed his rigid length and watched her eyes widen in surprise. "I want to feel your mouth on me, *cher*." Watching the pink tip of her tongue slide over the tip of his cock made his eyes roll so far back he lost sight of the beauty spread out in front of him. "That's it, lick the head. Mother of God and all things holy, I've died and gone to heaven."

He hoped like hell he didn't embarrass himself, but the warm wet touch of her velvet tongue circling the outer ridge of his corona was testing his control, unlike any blow job he'd ever had. Looking down, he was forced to lock his knees when she slid her hand down to his root before pulling it back to the top.

"I love that your touch isn't timid. Your grip is perfect, not too loose and not too tight. Jesus, Lord above, you are stealing my mind one stroke at a time." In the back recesses of his mind, Mitch knew Phoenix was fucking her—the pace of his thrusts picked up as he muttered a litany of curses. Phoenix groaned at the same time Aspen moaned, the sound vibrated against him and his cock swelled to the point Mitch wondered if it would burst.

He grasped the oversized bed's corner post as she slid him to the back of her throat and swallowed. Mitch felt her suck him down, pressing his cock against the roof of her mouth as his tip touched the back of her throat. "God dammit, I'm going to come, *cher*. If you don't…" he didn't get to finish his warning before she tightened both her hand and her lips leaving little doubt she planned to see it through to the end. Phoenix shouted her name and Aspen's entire body stiffened, her scream of release muffled by his cock pulsing seed down the back of her throat.

They'd all three come at the same time and even by BDSM standards that was damned impressive. He and Phoenix pulled from her, and Mitch grinned when she moaned in protest. Phoenix stepped into the small bathroom, and Mitch leaned down to press soft kisses over her face. "You rocked my world, baby. Holy shit, I had to lock my knees to keep from falling—your mouth is amazing."

He pulled back in time to see Phoenix lean over her with a washcloth. When she realized what he planned, she sat bolt upright, protesting. "I can do that. Geez, Louise. Give me that washcloth. Holy crapsters, how embarrassing is this? And I thought the Air Force pushed the boundaries…those people have no sense of modesty at all, I'm telling you. But dang, you weren't in the military, so I can't imagine what on Earth your excuse is. What would your sweet mama say if she saw you?"

She shuddered as Phoenix stood gaping at her completely flummoxed. The two of them stared at each other in confusion and Mitch laughed at loud. "You'd better stop talking while you're ahead, *cher*—although I'll admit, you aren't really ahead. More like just shy of completely sunk." Phoenix finally recovered from his surprise and frowned at Aspen before batting her hand away from the wet cloth he was holding.

"This is a part of our scene, little goddess. Rest assured, denying me this pleasure will not go well for you." As Phoenix patted her dry, someone pounded on the door so hard it actually rattled against the frame. They all three jumped and Aspen let out a yelp surprise. Phoenix glared at the door as if whoever had interrupted them could see him.

"What the fuck? What do you want?"

"Get your asses down to the office, we've got a problem." Mitch recognized Brandt Morgan's voice, but couldn't imagine what happened in the short time they'd been upstairs.

The change in Phoenix's demeanor was immediate. "Get dressed. I know that tone, and it always means trouble—*big trouble*."

PHOENIX WAS PISSED, and they hadn't even gotten to Nate's office yet. He'd struggled for a year to identify Athena, spent another couple of weeks planning tonight's activities down to a gnat's ass. And, now his brother decided to play Matt Fucking Dillon? What the hell could the Sheriff of Pine Creek be so wired up about? "Hell, this isn't even his jurisdiction. What crawled up his ass anyway?" He hadn't realized he'd spoken out loud until he heard Aspen giggle beside him.

It was good to hear the sweet tinkling sound of her laughter after the row she and Mitch had before leaving the private room. She'd insisted his order to "get dressed" included everything she would normally wear; Mitch claimed otherwise. Phoenix could have told her how their *discussion* was going to end, but he'd actually enjoyed watching them face-off. In the end, Mitch left the room with her panties in his pocket, and Aspen left the room with a bottom that was cherry red and would make her hiss the minute her ass cheeks connected with whatever flat surface they allowed her to sit on.

The sound of her voice re-centered his attention on the moment at hand. "Sure glad I'm not the only one who does that. People give me shit about it all the time. I just chalk it up to the fact I spend so much time alone." Something he could certainly relate to. His family ragged on him regularly that he needed to get out more. Even his sweet sister-in-law threatened to leave all three babies with him if he didn't crawl out of his hovel more often. And, there was a thought to strike terror in the heart of a grown man.

He loved his nieces to death, but babysitting them—all three of them? At the same time? It was just too terrifying to consider.

And now? Well, now it wouldn't be an issue because he planned to spend a lot more time outside his office because he had a sub who was in desperate need of training. But first, he had to deal with his brother and whatever crisis he'd managed to use to drag Phoenix away from the most spectacular sex he'd ever had. *God dammit it to hell, I'm going to kick his ass.*

ASPEN COULD PRACTICALLY feel the waves of tension radiating from Phoenix. She'd been relieved to hear him talking to himself because it made him seem far more human. She had to admit, found him more intimidating than she'd expected. Even though she was above average intellectually, she'd always seemed to attract men who weren't her intellectual equal...until now. Both Mitch and Phoenix were considered brilliant by anybody's standards, although Mitch seemed to make a concentrated effort to conceal it. Aspen suspected Phoenix didn't bother to mask his because he'd never worked outside of his family's compound and from what she'd read, they'd nurtured and encouraged his intellectual growth rather than feeling threatened by it.

Mitch tugged on her hand bringing her attention back to the moment. "I don't know where you went, *cher*, but I can't say I was pleased with the lost look on your pretty face. Come. Sit with me so we can find out what this is about." When she looked at the lone empty space on the sofa, she began looking around for another place for the two of them. He grinned at her and shook his head. "No, sweetness, this is where we'll sit. Come."

He couldn't possibly think the two of them would both fit in small space. She yelped in surprise when his large hand circled her wrist before he gave her a quick yank forward. "You are making a newbie sub mistake, *cher*. Your job is simple—trust your Dom to take care of you." He sat down and pulled her onto his lap.

BARRY COULDN'T BELIEVE he'd managed to elude the fucking moose who'd tried to tackle him outside the club. He'd barely managed to slip away by shedding his jacket and giving his pursuer a roundhouse kick to the side of the head. Recognizing the man as Taz Ledek, Barry felt a surge of pride when he turned the ignition switch and slammed the gear shift into drive. He'd cleared the curve before Ledek recovered enough to give chase and in another thirty seconds he was well beyond the reach of any of the club's staff.

He regretted losing his jacket simply because the night air was brisk enough that when he showed up without it at the small motel where he'd booked a room, it would make him stand out. With a little bit of luck, the snoopy old fart who usually manned the desk at night would be sleeping on the job again, and Barry could sneak by unnoticed.

It wasn't until he slipped into bed that he remembered the picture he'd left in his coat pocket. After a brief moment of panic, he smiled. Perhaps this evening hadn't been a loss after all. He hadn't been able to get Aspen pulled out the back door, but at least now Phoenix Morgan knew his lovely Athena was being targeted—it would only add to his torture. Barry would wait a couple of days before making contact, give the man time to stew in fear—it would undoubtedly make him much more agreeable when it came time to negotiate.

Yeah, that job definitely should have been his. He'd spent two years grooming himself for that promotion. Hell, the contacts alone would have netted him millions of dollars just for arranging access to government officials. Everything had been in fucking place until Phoenix Morgan got involved. The only piece of tonight's puzzle he couldn't figure out was why Aspen acted so confused when he'd called her Athena. Hell, he'd even given her his gamer name hoping she'd feel comfortable enough to step outside with him, but she'd still looked baffled. She should have known immediately who Maverick was, after all, they'd played Phoenix Morgan's games for almost a year. Hell, she'd even admitted his use of the Top Gun reference was what had first caught her attention. He hadn't bothered to tell her that was exactly why he'd chosen it.

At first, he'd thought she was the investigator who'd submarined him, but his boss had explained that she'd been brought in to do Morgan's secondary screen then replace him when the damned Montana cowboy was tapped for some top secret job by the big brass. It was just Barry's damned luck his own report had been one of only a handful Phoenix Morgan had completed. Evidently, the wheels in D.C. had given him a few promos to do so they could see just how deep he could dig, and in Barry's case, they'd gotten far more than they'd bargained for. They hadn't pulled his low level security clearance, but they'd damned well busted him back down so low on the totem pole they might as well have sent him to fucking Siberia.

Just a few more days and all those nasty police reports will disappear. Morgan will admit he made an error, and I'll be back in business. When he woke up, he'd sign on and see what sort of buzz was working through the gamers. If there was any news about Athena, that would be the first place it would turn up. *It can wait until I've slept a little.*

Chapter Fifteen

MITCH SHIFTED ASPEN so she was sitting at a right angle to his chest, and his hand moved in lazy circles over her lower back. Within a few minutes, he felt her relax, so it was almost time to wind her up a bit again. Phoenix had moved to the front of the room where he was conferring with his brother and Nate. Taz stood to the side of the room with what appeared to be an ice pack pressed to the side of his face. Holy hell, whoever was responsible for the bruise over Tashunka Ledek's temple had probably just signed their death warrant. Taz's expression was thunderous, and when Mitch finally caught his friend's attention, Taz gave him a quick hand signal for later.

Aspen's soft gasp of surprise let him know she'd seen the mark on Taz's face. When she started to stand, Mitch tightened his hold around her waist. "Sit still, *cher*. They'll give us a sit-rep in a minute until then I want you to stay exactly where I've put you. Master Phoenix is finding out what was so important his brother felt the need to interrupt our time together. Brandt Morgan is an experienced Dom; he wouldn't have disturbed us unless it was an emergency. But until we have the details, there is no reason to borrow trouble. And it gives me a chance to spend a little one-on-one time with you, so I'll count that as a bonus."

Mitch wasn't pleased Aspen's body language was once

again rigid, and her attention focused on Taz—something the other man hadn't missed. He gave Aspen a curt nod, before stepping to the other side of the men gathered around Nate's desk. Before his sweet sub could find another distraction, Mitch decided it was time to give her something else to focus on. Slipping his hand under the hem of her skirt, he began tracing slow, but deliberate circles over the soft skin covering her thighs. Using the pads of his fingers, he made sure he kept the pattern unpredictable while varying the intensity and speed. There was no doubt, keeping Aspen Andrews off base was going to be the only way to stay ahead of her.

Her breath hitched beautifully when he pushed his fingers higher. Even though he was still several inches from her sex, there'd be little question as to his intent. "Open for me, *cher*. I want to play with you while we wait. I promise we'll both enjoy the time much more than simply sitting here worrying about something we can't change."

"How do you know we can't change it?" Her voice was already edging toward that breathless sound he loved so much. It let him know she wasn't immune to his touch, even if she still hadn't opened as he'd commanded.

"Whatever it is has already happened, *cher*, and you and I both know we can't change the past. It's equally easy to see there are no immediate threats to your safety in this room, which removes the only possible reason I'd have to change my plan." He gave her several seconds to consider his words before reminding her about his earlier directive. "Now that I've explained myself—something you'll soon learn Doms don't particularly enjoy, is there some reason your knees are still clamped together?"

She immediately released the pressure but didn't slide her knees apart until he leveled a look at her letting her know his patience was waning quickly. She moved her legs apart so slightly he might not have noticed if she hadn't been sitting on his lap. Hell, feeling the insignificant move was the only indication he had she'd made any attempt to comply. "Are you deliberately being obtuse, *cher*? Because, as I'm sure you can see, my hands are not going to fit comfortably in that small space. This is your last warning, open for me. I want to play with you."

She finally voiced the objection he'd already known she was trying valiantly to hold back. "But there are other people in the room. They'll know what we're doing even if my skirt covers your hand. And holy craptastic, Jax is here, what will he think?" Her words were coming faster and her voice raising in pitch letting him know she was skating perilously close to panic by the time she paused long enough to take a breath. "I'll get the lecture of all lectures. It'll probably be worse than the one I got before my first date, and God knows that was one for record books. Holy Hannah, I wondered for a while if they were going to send me to a convent. I should have never mentioned that by the way because Kent whistled various songs from *The Sound of Music* every time I mentioned having a date the entire time I was in college. I swear he only quit because I threatened to talk to Lilly. To this day, I want to cry every time I see it's coming on television because I know he'll send me reminders."

Mitch couldn't hold back any longer, he burst out laughing. He wasn't sure which was the most amusing, the fact Kent West knew enough about the movie to whistle the tunes or that threatening to tell his mother made him stop teasing her, at least temporarily. Either way, it pleased him she was exhibiting small signs of personal trust. In his experience, women will only babble about their frustration to people they trust. The women he'd been involved with were usually more than willing to voice complaints when they were warranted, but the stream of consciousness chatter was reserved for those in their inner circle.

He might not be thrilled with her reservations about playing in front of the other Doms, but he did understand it. "I can assure you, Jax will move if it bothers him. Remember, your friends are Doms. And yes, they will know exactly what we're doing because it's what they would expect. I assure you, if both Jax and Micah are in a room with Gracie, one of them is going to have his hands on her during a meeting." And wasn't that the understatement of the year? He could guarantee her friends would play openly with their lovely Latina sub because he'd seen it time and time again.

"Here are your options. Obey the command and open your legs so I can enjoy feeling those lovely pink folds. I'll bet they are soaked despite your attempts to stall and convince me you don't want to feel my touch. Or, you can continue on this path and see how quickly it lands you face down over my lap. How much happier will Jax be to see my hand leaving scarlet prints all over your bare ass cheeks?"

"You wouldn't." There wasn't any outrage in her voice, but she didn't believe he'd punish her in front of everyone in the room. She was wrong.

"Are you confident enough in your theory to test it, *cher*? Because I assure you, I am definitely up to the task. I can promise you, every other Dom in the room has already taken notice of our prolonged discussion, and they'll be expecting my patience to end very, very soon." He watched as her eyes darted around the room, noting each of the men glancing their way at various points.

Mitch knew when her gaze met Phoenix's—her soft gasp and the quick catch in her respiration meant she hadn't missed the lust in the man's eyes. "I can tell by the way your body is responding, you've seen the desire in your other Master's eyes. Remember, the submissive always holds the reins—submission is all about trust, and our desire is fed by yours." He loved the way her pulse throbbed at the base of her throat, it told him everything he needed to know about the way his words were affecting her.

When he felt her take a deep breath before relaxing against him, Mitch knew he'd won the first battle. There was little doubt she'd test them again, hell, she'd probably test them every single day. It was ironic really. He'd never been drawn to subs who weren't already trained, and he knew Phoenix was of a like mind, but there was something about her that drew him like a moth to a flame. He'd felt the pull the first time he'd seen her, and it hadn't abated in the intervening months.

Aspen might feel like she'd done her homework, but there was a stark difference between reading about the lifestyle and actually immersing yourself in it. The rules often seemed arbitrary to newbies, but each and every rule he and Phoenix would insist she follow would have a very specific purpose. There would be times the only purpose of a rule was to ensure she maintained a certain level of discipline, but more often than not, rules were in place to insure her safety.

As far as Mitch was concerned, every Dom's number one responsibility was to cherish and protect his submissive. As his friends would attest, it wasn't always a popular position to be in, but that would never change the fact safety trumped all other concerns. But right now, safety wasn't an issue, and she was deliberately holding back, so it was time to explain exactly where her hesitance had gotten her.

"I think you are far more interested in playing in front of an audience than you're owning up to. You may not even be willing to admit it to yourself yet, but I'm going to show you how much fun playing in front of others can be." She stiffened against him again, but this time, her eyes were alight with desire rather than hesitance.

"We still have time to play a bit before they start talking to us about anything important." With those words, Mitch turned her so her back was against his chest and pulled the front of her pleated skirt up to the top of her thighs. Hooking his feet around her ankles it was easy to pull her legs apart exposing her bare sex to everyone standing in front of them. Phoenix's eyes flashed an enflamed look in her direction and Mitch wanted to laugh at the curse he saw his friend utter.

"Lean back, *cher*, I'm going to play with you. Watch your other Master's reaction. See the fire in his eyes—how difficult we are making it for him to concentrate on what his brother is saying? By the time this little infomercial is over, nothing will keep him from barging over here and claiming his share of the fun. You'll be lucky if he doesn't throw you over his shoulder and haul your delectable ass upstairs like a fucking caveman." Mitch had seen Kent torment Kyle in much the same way more than once during meetings. By the time, Kyle had wrapped things up he'd been almost out of control until he'd gotten his fill of Tobi.

The West brothers were well known for public play and had only afforded their lovely sub moderate levels of privacy throughout her first pregnancy. He wasn't sure the two Doms would have been so open to revealing her changing body if she hadn't fussed with them continually about it. The more she fought them, the more they pushed her. Most of the other Doms at the Prairie Winds Club had never seen a pregnant woman in all her naked glory, so it had been a learning experience for many of them as well. Brian and Kirk swore Kent and Kyle had done the younger men a huge favor by allowing them to see the beauty of a woman's rounded form. Since many of those same Doms had wives and were now planning families of their own, they'd be much better prepared for the changes they'd see.

Shoving all those thoughts aside, Mitch grinned at Phoenix's obvious frustration, earning him a glacial glare. Sliding his fingers through Aspen's soft folds, he drew slow circles around her swollen clit as he pressed kisses to the soft spot below her ear. "You're deliciously wet for me, *cher*. I can't begin to tell you how much I love knowing you're enjoying this bit of exhibition. Playing in public is one of my very favorite things, and I'm going to enjoy playing with you on one of the stages downstairs. Knowing Phoenix and I are the envy of every Dom in the room will add to our pleasure."

Aspen's body was slowly relaxing as her arousal began blocking out any residual embarrassment she might be feeling. Her soft moans were going to shatter his control. If he didn't bring her to release quickly, there was going to be a serious change in the tone of this meeting. The woman was simply too tempting.

"You slay me, *cher*. Everything about you draws me like a magnet to steel. Your hips lifting into my touch, the feel of your cream coating my fingers as I let them slide through your swollen folds—baby, you are a Dom's wet dream come to life." Cupping her cheek with his large palm, Mitch turned her into his kiss, capturing her cries as he pinched her pulsing clit sending her over the top.

Easing her down from what seemed like an earth-shattering release took several minutes as she lay shuddering against his chest. Phoenix brought over one of the club's soft subbie blankets making no attempt to hide his straining erection. Wrapping it around her, he leaned down and took her lips in a forceful kiss. "You chose your name well, sweetness. You're a fucking goddess when you come. As soon as we're finished here, we're going to head up to the ranch."

Mitch gave his friend an inquiring look, but Phoenix gave him a quick shake of his head before mouthing *later*. Obviously, whatever happened involved Aspen's safety, it was the only reason Mitch could think of Phoenix would be willing to wait to take her. What he didn't know was what the hell the holdup was. "What or who are we waiting for?"

An emotion Mitch couldn't identify crossed his friend's face before Phoenix seemed back to business. "Kip. Or more specifically, Caila Cooper. It seems the Mistress of Mayhem has once again managed to land herself in a peck of trouble." Mitch had heard the Morgan brothers talk about their neighbor *girl* but hadn't dreamt she was old enough to have been admitted to Mountain Mastery.

"Your neighbor? Why was she here? And where is she now?"

"It seems Caila managed to grow up while none of us were watching. And from what I've heard, Kip pulled her upstairs an hour ago and despite Brandt's threats to breakdown the door, little brother doesn't seem to give a rat's ass the rest of us are left down here cooling our heels while he plays knight in shining armor." It was easy to see there was more to the story, but Mitch decided those questions could wait. If he had to guess, he figured the older Morgan brothers were worried their youngest brother's reputation as a one-night wonder would hurt the young women they were all so fond of.

Brandt had told him once that Calamity was the closest thing they had to a little sister, so it was easy to see why Phoenix was so frustrated with Kip. Mitch's throbbing erection pressing relentlessly against the zipper of his pants made him silently curse the youngest Morgan as well. *Get your ass down here kid, waiting isn't my best trait.*

Chapter Sixteen

PHOENIX WATCHED KIP swagger into the room followed by a dazed looking Caila. He wanted to slap the smirk off his brother's face and remind him of the importance of aftercare. *Jesus, Joseph, and Mary, he isn't even holding her hand. I'm going to kick his ass.* From the scowl on Brandt's face, Phoenix wasn't the only one unhappy with their younger brother.

"Now that Kip has finally decided to bring Caila back downstairs, we'll get started." Brandt's tone left little question about how frustrated he was with Kip's cavalier attitude. "Caila, please tell us every detail you remember about the man you accosted you." Phoenix watched as she blinked her eyes several times trying to focus on Brandt's request. Every Dom in the room recognized the signs, she was still trying to battle her way back from the haze of what must have been a marathon sex scene. The post-orgasmic haze in her eyes would clear much quicker with the appropriate after-care, and now Nate was also glaring at Kip.

Surprising them all, Joelle stepped up to Kip and poked him in the chest as she spoke. "What the hell, Kip? You're being a jerk. Where the heck is the sweet brother-in-law Coral, Josie, and I all love? Where is the guy who is always so supportive of the three of us when our men make us crazy? I don't like this change at all. You're being an arrogant prick, and if no one else is going to say what we're all thinking, then I will."

Holy shit! Phoenix wanted to applaud and from the looks on the faces of the others in the room, he wasn't the only one. Ryan took measured steps forward until he was able to shackle Joelle's wrist, as he faced down his cousin. "She's right, Kip, even though I find her timing a bit disturbing." Looking at his lovely wife, he grinned. "You'll get a paddling for talking to another Dom so disrespectfully at the club, my darling sub—even though I doubt it will be much of a punishment."

If Phoenix knew his cousin, he planned to reward Joelle's courage while disguising it as a punishment. Damn, you had to love his creativity. Joelle muttered, "It was worth it. He's being an asshat. Wait until Coral gets wind of this." Phoenix chuckled, and several others in the room coughed in an effort to cover their own laughter. Joelle's parting shot mentioning Coral made Kip cringe, no doubt their oldest brother's lovely wife would take an even dimmer view of Kip's inconsiderate behavior.

Nate brought everyone's attention back to the matter at hand by brushing past Kip and pulling Caila into his arms. "Sweetness, come here for a minute." When she started to step back, he shook his head. "No. Be still and let me hold you. I want to make sure you're all right, and I need to calm down before I say something to Master Kip I'll regret later."

Kip might not be as committed to the lifestyle as the other Morgans, but it was clear from the chastised look on his face, he realized he'd pushed the boundary too far. Landing on Nate's shit list wasn't an enviable position for a Dom or a submissive. *Yeah, little brother's definitely gotten his ass in the fire.*

By the time Caila finished describing her assailant, Aspen was fully focused, and Phoenix could tell she was barely holding back what he was sure was going to be a barrage of questions. It was only after Aspen approached Calamity that he noticed how similar the two women were in size and physical appearance. They were almost exactly the same height and body build, their hair color was nearly identical and cut in similar styles, although Caila's was longer. The biggest difference he could see was the color of their eyes and the fact that Ms. Cooper was easily five years younger.

Turning to Brandt, he quietly asked the question he wasn't sure he wanted the answer to. "You think he mistook Caila for Aspen, don't you?" The regret he saw in his brother's eyes was all the answer he needed. "Fuck. I don't even want to think about how this is going to affect Aspen, she's going to feel awful thinking she's put someone else in danger."

"I figured. She knew the risks when she signed on with DHS, but Caila is innocent in this mess. Honestly, I was worried this was where we were headed when we found Aspen's picture in the man's pocket. But hell, even I didn't realize how much they look alike until I saw them standing side-by-side—it would have been an easy mistake to make, especially if you didn't know either of them really well."

Just then Caila straightened and went white as a sheet. To Kip's credit, he was the first to her side. "What is it, Cal?" Kip only shortened their nickname for her when he was worried about her and Phoenix was glad to see he seemed to have snapped out of his earlier self-absorption.

"I just remembered, he said something about wishing it had been me who'd done his paperwork. He acted like I should know what he meant, but I was too scared to ask what he was talking about." When she shuddered, Kip pulled her close, draping his arm over her shoulders in a move Phoenix knew she'd recognize. The light in Caila's eyes dimmed when she realized Kip was pushing her gently back into the neighbor box. *Damn.* He wanted to slap some good sense into his younger brother. Kip should have never taken her unless he was prepared to follow through. It was a real prick move to view Caila as casually as he typically looked at other women.

Brandt looked up from the picture in his hands, smiling indulgently at the young woman they all still saw as a kid. "Anything else, Caila? Close your eyes and try to picture it again in your mind, but I also want you to hold on to Kip's hand. Let him keep you grounded while you go back in your mind." Phoenix watched as she let Kip take her hand as she closed her eyes. Her expression quickly shifted from the affable look she'd given Brandt, the small frown lines appearing between her brows indicating her concern with whatever she was reliving.

When she shuddered, Kip's soft curse let Phoenix know his brother was more invested in the situation than he appeared. Letting go of her hand to wrap his arm around her shoulder, Phoenix watched as she unconsciously leaned into Kip's hold. When her eyes flew open, it was Phoenix she turned to. "He called me Athena...isn't that the name of the woman who kicks your ass in your games? I don't play often, but I've seen enough on-line chatter to know there is a lot of speculation about you and Mitch and the player named after some Greek goddess."

Nate stepped behind her giving her ass a sharp swat rocking her up on her toes. "Check the attitude, precious. You are still in a BDSM club and the rules about respect apply in the office just as they do the rest of the facility.

You're skating very close to the edge, and since you don't have a Dom, I won't think twice about giving you the spanking you deserve." Kip might not be ready to commit himself to Caila, but the icy look he gave Nate spoke volumes.

Before Phoenix could react to everything happening around him, Aspen had wiggled away from Mitch and planted herself squarely in front of Caila. "Oh my God, he almost hurt you because he thought you were me. Are you okay, sweetie? Holy crapping cottontails, I can't believe this."

Caila blinked a couple of times before laughing. "Seriously? You're Athena? What kind of blind bastard mistakes you for me? Good heavens, you're gorgeous."

Another resounding slap of Nate's palm against a barely covered ass had the other Dom's in the room chuckling. In typical Brandt Morgan fashion, Phoenix saw his brother grin as he arched a brow at his longtime friend. "Damn, Nate, you're losing control of the submissives in this club at an alarming rate. You may need to call in reinforcements if Tobi or Coral show up." When Joelle glared at her husband, his smile widened. "Go ahead and say it, minx, I've been looking for a good excuse to wear out that pretty ass of yours."

Joelle's pout was pretty and likely all the excuse Brandt needed to lay some crimson stripes over his sweet sub's ass. Phoenix knew his lovely sister-in-law had been so busy recently she probably hadn't had time to get in enough trouble to suit Brandt—the middle Morgan brother loved nothing more than having her bare ass draped over his lap. Ryan pulled her back into his arms and sighed. "Baby, I have a different vision for this evening, so please try to refrain from poking the bear."

Phoenix refocused his attention on Aspen's frantic inquiries about whether or not Caila was sure she was all right. Pulling Aspen back against his chest, Phoenix wrapped his arm around her low, so when he slid it up under her breasts, he lifted the front of her dress enough she'd feel even the slightest brush of air move over her exposed sex. Any movement she made would have her flashing everyone in the room. Leaning down, he spoke against the soft shell of her ear. "If Caila tells you she is okay, she is. She may be young, but she's wicked smart, and she trusts us enough to tell us if she'd been injured."

"Oh yeah, I've had plenty of experience running to the Morgan brothers when I got hurt...really, lots and lots of experience. Besides, I don't want to get paddled by Master Nate for telling a lie...I've seen how that works out for subs, and it's not pretty." Nate's smug look made Phoenix want to laugh, the little minx had managed to assure Aspen she was okay and stroke the club owner's ego all in one go. Hell, even he had to admire her diplomatic efforts. And she was right, she'd had a lifetime's experience confessing her dangerous escapades to them. *I've never met anyone who can get themselves into as much trouble as the Mistress of Mayhem.*

ASPEN'S HEAD WAS spinning with a thousand questions as she stood in front of the stunning little blonde who'd entered a few minutes ago with Kip Morgan. Since she'd been talking to Phoenix for months on-line, it didn't take her long to identify the Morgan's neighbor despite the fact she'd been confused at first. The way Phoenix had always spoken about her, Aspen had assumed Calamity was much younger. *Anybody talking to Jax, Kent, or Kyle about me*

probably thinks I'm still in junior high, so I don't know why I'm surprised.

She was worried the younger woman was concealing how badly she'd been traumatized by the events, but when Phoenix wrapped his arm around her, Aspen pushed her concerns aside. When cool air moved against her bare sex, her attention shifted quickly. Standing perfectly still was the only way she was going to avoid another peep show during the meeting intended to keep Caila safe.

Hoping her sincerity showed in her expression, Aspen spoke quietly to the sweet young woman leaning into Kip's hold. "I'm so sorry, Caila. Please know, I'd never have come here if I'd had any idea he'd follow me to Montana."

As soon as the words left her lips, Aspen knew she'd made a mistake. Phoenix's arm suddenly felt like a band of steel, the difference a few seconds could make was truly remarkable. His hold had gone from seduction to restraint in the time it took her to open her big mouth. *Damn it, when will I ever learn to keep my mouth shut. They'll likely be pissed as hell I've brought trouble to their door...and who can blame them?*

Mitch moved to stand in front of her so quickly he was practically a blur of motion. "What did you just say, *cher*? What sort of trouble have you had prior to your arrival?" When she didn't answer immediately, he pinched her nipples firmly enough to make her gasp. "Stop thinking and answer the question without all the mental editing."

"Mental editing?"

Another sharp pinch made her squeak. "I know full well you are trying to figure out exactly how much you could say, how much you should reveal. Let me help you with that decision. Tell us all of it. Now." His tone left little question about how serious he was. This was obviously not a command she would be wise to ignore. *Choose your battles, Aspen.*

"I've known for a while someone was stalking Phoenix through his games, but I haven't been able to back-trace him. Whoever he is, he's really careful and has managed to stay one step ahead of me at every turn." She saw several of the men in the room glancing at each other. *Great now they think I'm some sort of loon.*

Taking a deep breath, there wasn't anything to do but forge ahead. "The thing is…after I'd done the initial report on Phoenix for DHS, I continued playing the on-line games because I enjoyed the on-line banter." Returning her attention to Mitch, Aspen smiled up into his surprised face. "At first, I thought you were another profile Phoenix had created because your *voice*, the way you phrase things, etc., is so similar and you were rarely gaming at the same time. But I finally spent some time following your cyber trail and found out who you were."

Grinning at Micah Drake's thunderous expression, Aspen shook her head. "Don't get all pissy. Your programs are good…hell, they're really good. But I found the back door so you might want to lock that baby up. And, no, I didn't share that information with my supervisor." *Who am I kidding? I probably won't even have a job after tonight. Ichabod will be overjoyed to have me out of his hair.* Her boss hadn't been thrilled to have her pushed onto his team. Robert Crane had been even less happy to learn of her connections to Kent and Kyle West, but she hadn't cared enough about his complaints to explore his reasoning. *Yeah, and how is THAT working out for you?*

The silence in the room was deafening, and her face heated from the continued scrutiny. Brandt Morgan was staring at her, obviously trying to decide whether or not she was somehow responsible for what happened to Caila. "Why exactly *are* you here, Captain?" His use of her former title wasn't a slip, and she knew it. He was deliberately putting a huge chasm of professional distance between them. It was a jerk move, but she wasn't going to call him on it.

"Well, Sheriff Morgan." *See? Two can play your game, asshole.* "I like your brother. We had a great rapport online, and I didn't want to see him hurt. And, I'd already met Mitch, and as I'm sure you already know, because of unfortunate timing, we didn't get to explore what I felt was a mutual attraction...so, I saw this as a second chance with him."

"But why now? The timing seems suspect to me," Brandt's voice was tight, and she fought back the temptation to tell him to focus on what was important...the young woman trembling in Kip's arms.

"I wanted to meet Phoenix and thought the club would be my best opportunity." Jax was the only one in the room who seemed convinced she'd answered honestly. He'd known her long enough to recognize when she was lying or telling the truth. "I wanted to keep your brother safe because I'd come to see him as a friend...and...well, I don't really have many friends. And my three best friends have gotten married and had families of their own."

Stiffening her spine and putting up her hand to stay him when she saw Jax take a step forward, she looked directly into Brandt's eyes. "From what I've read in your file, Sheriff, you probably understand what it's like to have too few friends. And I'll bet you've seen some of those fade when your buddies' lives changed from fellow soldiers and teammates to husbands and fathers. It isn't bad or unfair, it's just the way things work."

Brandt studied her carefully, but she held her ground. Aspen saw the light in his eyes shift the moment he decided she'd passed muster. The slow accepting smile spreading over his face totally transformed his appearance. *Holy hotness, no wonder Joelle was watching him with worshipful eyes.* "Welcome to Montana, Captain." This time, the title sounded more like an endearment, and she wondered if she hadn't just gained a nickname. *Yippy Skippy.*

BRANDT WASN'T AN easy sell when it came to the safety of his family and friends. But, the pretty blonde Phoenix and Mitch were flanking with mirrored protective poses hadn't hesitated to stand up to him when he'd questioned her. Jax had watched from the sidelines, and his relaxed posture helped convince him Aspen Andrews was telling the truth. Brandt found it damned amusing she'd come to Montana intending to protect Phoenix—something he was more than happy to take off her plate.

He'd watched the former Air Force pilot continue to fuss over Caila, her concern for their young neighbor easy to see. He'd been damned amused by the way her spine straightened when she knew he was questioning her motives. Yeah, she would definitely fit in with the other Morgan women. Giving himself a mental shake for the leap forward his thoughts had just taken, Brandt stepped back letting Jax take over.

"Sweetheart, Micah is going to want to talk to you sooner rather than later."

"Fuck yeah," Micah's muttered agreement from the side sent a ripple of laughter through the room.

"And Kent, Kyle, and I are all going to have a long chat

with you as well. I'm damned interested in knowing why you didn't call us about that fucking back door." Brandt knew Jax McDonald well enough to know the computer issue wasn't as important as the other issue she'd eluded to, and his suspicion was confirmed when Jax stepped up and pulled Aspen into a crushing hug. "But most of all, I want to know why you didn't tell your three dimwitted friends how left out you felt. Baby girl, you know hurting you is the very last thing any of us would ever do intentionally."

Brandt watched her body shaking as she sobbed, the overload of emotion and adrenaline drop finally getting the best of her. Phoenix watched from the sideline for a few seconds before stepping forward and pulling her into his own embrace. *Good man.*

Chapter Seventeen

STARING BLANKLY THROUGH the windshield of Phoenix's pickup, Aspen wondered again how she'd let herself be coerced into leaving her car behind. Brandt had assured her he'd see to it her small rental made its way to the ranch "soon" which she knew translated to *when my brother deems it necessary*. *Damn*. There wasn't much she hated more than being dependent on someone else for a ride. The feeling of being stranded always set her nerves on edge.

Mitch's large hand pressed down on her leg halting the nervous bounce she hadn't even been aware of. "You are wound awfully tight, *cher*. Care to enlighten us as to why?"

Muttering under her breath, Aspen cursed the fact Doms were so damned observant. "Is that a real question or was it rhetorical?" His low growl was her answer and with an audible sigh, she made a concentrated effort to calm her rising panic. "I'm not comfortable going to someone else's home without my own vehicle." What she'd said was true, but it certainly wasn't the whole story.

Phoenix's soft chuckle beside her made Aspen turn in his direction. "I'm sorry, sweetness, but that excuse was about as transparent as they come. I'm translating it to read, *I want to be able to bolt if things get too intense*." His eyes left the road long enough to give her a knowing look before returning his focus to the straight stretch of highway they were barreling down.

"Don't you have to drive the speed limit? Or do you get some sort of special consideration because your brother is the sheriff?" Her deflection probably wouldn't work, but what the hell, it was worth a shot. She knew her irritation with his driving was misplaced, but she really didn't care. After working with men for her entire adult life, she'd learned a long time ago there was no reason to even attempt to explain her emotions. More often than not, her friends and coworkers looked at her like she'd grown a second head when she tried to explain her almost irrational fear of being trapped without a way out.

When Phoenix and Mitch exchanged looks over the top or her head, Aspen became even more annoyed. "Stop with the silent communication you don't think I'm noticing. The guys have always done that, and it never helps my mood." The truth was, it pissed her off, but she wasn't willing to cop to something they might eventually use against her.

After everything that had happened tonight, she simply hadn't had the strength to fight them on the car issue. And Phoenix's promise to paddle her bare ass in front of everyone if she didn't stop arguing had been equal parts annoying and arousing—another point of dissention pissing her off.

"We'll be at the ranch in twenty minutes. Until then, we'll table this discussion. I think we'll be able to sort this out pretty quickly when you understand the consequences for snark and evasion." His smug tone made her want to deny the effect his Dominance was having on her body. But, she knew that would be tantamount to waving a red flag in front of a couple of bulls. Crossing her arms over her chest and slumping back against the seat, she tried to distract herself from the throbbing pulsing in her sex. *Damn it to donuts, there's no way I'll be able to deny how turned on I am if either of them decides to slide the hands resting on my knees further up my thighs.*

As if she'd *thought his actions into existence*, Mitch's hand slid up until the tips of his fingers traced over the soaking folds with touches so light, Aspen caught herself lifting her hips trying to move closer to intensify the sensation. "I think our sub needs some distraction. She's thinking too much. The problem with smart women is they get all tied up with a zillion things bouncing around in their minds, and they forget all about taking care of themselves. They disregard their own needs to please others."

Aspen wondered how he'd known she was getting stuck in a quagmire of guilt and fear, but the tighter his fingertips pressed against her soaking sex, the less she could concentrate on anything but the building pleasure. Heat streaked from her sex like lightning bolts, the electricity traveling up her spine before arcing all the way to the tips of her toes and fingers. Losing herself in the vortex swirling around her was more appealing than sorting out her feelings, so she let go.

MITCH KNEW THE moment Aspen surrendered because her entire body seemed to sag with relief. He loved that moment with subs. It was always special, but the first time they experienced it was usually something they never forgot. Hell, he didn't even regret the fact they were in a fucking pick-up driving up a mountain road in darkness so intense it felt like nothing existed outside the truck. Perhaps the intimacy was enhanced because of their close proximity? He wasn't sure. All he knew was how beautiful Aspen looked as she let him lead her to a whole new place where nothing mattered but pleasure.

When she slumped back in the seat, gasping for breath, he couldn't resist releasing her seat belt and pulling her onto his lap. They were only a mile from the ranch's main house and they both needed a moment to get themselves together before facing whatever chaos was currently taking place inside the Morgan Mansion.

He'd been an only child, and he'd longed for entertainment siblings would have provided. Perhaps that was why Mitch loved visiting the Morgans? Hell, there was always *something* happening, and often it was full-blown pandemonium. With so many people living on the property and nearby, somebody was always around whether you were looking for conversation or a co-conspirator. The main house was massive, but he'd been impressed by how homey the space felt.

One wing served as a home for Sage, Coral, and their three toddlers. Faith, Hope, and Charity Morgan were already *large and in-charge* as their mama described them. Mitch wondered how much more bedlam would ensue when they were teens. And what sort of influence would those three hellions have on the cousins who were sure to join the Morgan family soon? Suppressing the full body shudder threatening to surface, he considered the population explosion he was sure was lurking just around the corner. Mitch pushed aside his current train of thought.

The front door opened, as they parked in front of the house and Mitch wasn't surprised to see Sage Morgan descending the wide stone steps. Nodding to Aspen, Sage shook his head when she offered her hand. Tensing beside her, Mitch had a split second of panic before Sage pulled

Aspen into a crushing hug. "I want to thank you for looking out for my little brother, Aspen. It's a damned big job watching out for the four of them, and I'm grateful for your help—hell, I want to kiss the ground Josie and Joelle walk on most days."

Mitch could hear the emotion in the man's voice even though he was trying to make light of the situation. One thing he knew about the Morgans—they were often each other's most vocal critics, but they were also their strongest supporters. Phoenix punched his brother in the arm and growled, "You've already got a woman, leave ours alone."

Sage grinned at Aspen when he released her. "You've got your work cut out for you, Captain." Aspen's eyes sparked with recognition and Mitch grinned. Evidently, Brandt's pet name for her was going to stick. "Come on inside, let's get you out of the night air." Sage froze for a minute and then shook his head laughing. "Holy hell, I sound like Dad. Damn, I wasn't expecting that to happen for a few years yet."

Since the eldest Morgan sibling hadn't released Aspen, Mitch and Phoenix trailed behind. Phoenix's muttered, "It's not a surprise to anybody else, he's thought he was our second dad ever since I can remember." Aspen's giggle let them know she and Sage hadn't missed Phoenix's snarky remark.

"Careful Geek-Boy or I'll tell Coral you graciously volunteered to babysit this weekend to give us a weekend off. She's been hinting about a shopping trip to Denver, but with Mom and Dad back down south, and Josie on tour, our usual back-up team isn't available." Mitch had seen then havoc three toddlers could wreck and could well imagine it taking four adults to keep up with them.

"Not happening, brother. I'm going to be busy." The

grin on Phoenix's face made Mitch laugh out loud.

Mitch nodded in agreement. "Yeah, Romeo, you're on your own this weekend and probably next weekend as well." Personally, Mitch couldn't imagine giving up time in Aspen's bed to chase after the girls—at least not in the near future. *Maybe when they are all potty trained…no, by then they'll probably have learned how to open doors and who knows what sort of mischief they'd get into then. Face it, those girls are going to be a challenge for years.*

PHOENIX HADN'T SAID anything to Aspen, but while she'd been enjoying Mitch's aftercare in the truck, his phone had been lighting up like the fucking Fourth of July with alerts as they drove through the gates to the ranch. The security system he'd installed included a state of the art system designed to identify and block any monitoring device.

His business was so competitive; Phoenix simply could not risk anyone spying—either intentionally or unintentionally. More than once, he'd discovered *bugs* in the purses and bags of friends and family he knew were completely unaware. The technology was so sophisticated and the devices so small, they could easily be slipped in without the owners' knowledge. Hell, his own mom's purse had been bugged several times.

It was going to be interesting to see who'd been so interested in where Aspen was headed they'd taken the chance of putting a tracker in her purse or luggage. There was always a chance it was an agency device, but Phoenix doubted it. He'd put enough tagged word searches in her agency's system, he'd know before she did if he was being spied on. But, he had to admit it chapped his ass that she'd known he was being stalked in his own games, and he'd been clueless. *Maybe if I hadn't been so focused on finding her, I'd have noticed.*

Phoenix listened as she and Sage made small talk while his oldest brother made them all something to drink. He fought back his frustration—fucking hell, he didn't want to sit down here chit-chatting with his damned brother. He wanted to be in his suite with Aspen naked and screaming his name.

When Mitch started playing with her in the truck, Phoenix had nearly driven off the road more than once. The scent of her arousal filled the truck's cab, and his cock responded with the most painful erection of his life. The only way the torture could have been worse would have been if he'd been forced to watch without being able to participate. Hell, listening had been almost enough to have him coming in his jeans like a damned teenager.

Aspen kept glancing at him while she feigned listening to Sage babble about his upcoming trip to Texas. Evidently, his brother assumed Aspen would be interested since she'd grown up in the Lone Star state. What the hell was wrong with Sage? Was he so desperate to talk to a woman he was willing to talk endlessly to the woman Phoenix was currently fantasizing about bending over the coffee table so he could fuck her until they were both mindless? Hell, in another minute or two he wouldn't care if his entire family watched. They could call out suggestions or throw money if it made them happy, he wouldn't care.

"He's only talking her up because he's enjoying watching the steam come out your ears. If you'd stop growling at him, Sage would go back upstairs. I'm sure your sister-in-law would thank you. The last time she looked over the bannister, I swore she was going to throw what I suspect was a rancid diaper. Considering how FUBAR tonight has become, I'm sure one of us would most certainly get nailed."

"She wouldn't dare. I swear I'd paddle her ass myself."

"You could try." Coral's amused voice came from behind him, and Phoenix glared at Mitch who was trying valiantly to hold back his laughter.

"You're a real ass, you know that, Mitch? First, that little show in the truck and now this? Are you deliberately trying to provoke me?" Phoenix was already picturing their next sparring session in the gym. Phoenix might not have been in the Special Forces, but having three older brothers was training enough for what he had in mind for his best friend.

"I don't know, Mitch, I've seen that look before, and it usually proceeds somebody getting their ass handed to them in the ring. You don't have a gym session planned in the near future, do you? Because I'm pretty sure you should probably consider rescheduling it if you do." When Phoenix turned with slow deliberation to face Coral she glanced nervously up at him. "Hey, I was just kidding, you know that, right?"

Phoenix narrowed his eyes at her and took a menacing step forward. "Big brother, your cheeky sub seems to have forgotten she lives in a house with more than one Dom."

"Is that so? Well, you know I've always told you guys not to wait for me to handle disrespectful behavior." The underlying tone of amusement broke through Phoenix's haze of frustration, and he watched as Coral visibly paled. "It takes a village to raise a child, and it seems that same axiom also applies to keeping a submissive in line."

Phoenix had never spanked his beloved sister-in-law for misbehaving, and he wasn't about to delay his own plans with Aspen to give Coral the punishment she deserved. But that didn't mean he wasn't enjoying the wide-eyed look she was giving him.

"Look, think about this for a minute. Who would take care of the girls if I was too sore to sit down and rock them to back to sleep? Joelle is trying to make a baby of her own, and Mom Morgan is probably sipping wine and watching the waves crash ashore someplace warm…the traitor. Josie is wrapping up another tour, and we all know what that means…they'll lock themselves in a ritzy suite in Hawaii and nobody will see them for a week. And you haven't even introduced me to Aspen yet, so it seems cruel to hand off the Morgan Menaces to someone unsuspecting."

Her voice was raising in pitch the longer she spoke, her nervousness growing exponentially. *Good.* He'd help Sage scene with Coral a few times in their basement dungeon, but he'd always refused to mete out any punishment—a decision he might need to revisit. "Perhaps I'll just tell Brandt you've spilled the beans about them starting a family."

Everyone knew how notoriously private the middle Morgan brother was, knowing Joelle had shared something so personal with Coral—who'd then blurted it out to save her own sweet ass would get both subs in hot water. "Oh shit…umm, I mean, don't do that…it wouldn't be fair to Joelle. You know how Brandt is…"

"Oh, indeed I do. But I have to admit, I'm looking forward to being an uncle again, so I'm not particularly inclined to stall their progress. But, then again, you do both need to learn to stop gossiping." Like that was ever going to happen, the three Morgan wives were as thick as thieves, and their husbands wouldn't have it any other way.

Sage moved in front of his lovely wife, arms crossed over his chest and gave her a look Phoenix recognized well. The last time she'd elicited that particular look from her Dom, he'd flogged her on the cross to the precipice of orgasm time and time again until she'd finally broken down and sobbed for relief. The rest of the play party had broken up by the time he'd finally let her come, but Sage swore Coral's scream had broken the sound barrier.

"I swear, I don't know what I'm going to do with you, pet, but I'm up to the challenge. You better start thinking of ways to keep from waking those girls up until I'm finished reminding you of the rules." He'd already thrown her over his shoulder before turning to give Aspen a playful wink. Phoenix saw her shoulders drop as she relaxed. He hadn't considered she'd think Coral was really in trouble.

Sage swatted Coral's ass as he bounded up the stairs, but they could still hear her surprised shriek. "Quiet, wench, you don't want the children to witness your punishment, do you?" They disappeared down the hall.

Aspen stared at the top of the stair for several seconds before turning her wide green eyes to him. "Is she going to be okay? I can't believe you got her in trouble." Mitch chuckled beside her, and she turned her piercing look on him. "And you didn't do a thing to help her, either. What the hell? I thought Doms were supposed to be super protective? Geez, I've heard Tobi and Gracie complain endlessly about how over-protective all the Doms at Prairie Winds are...maybe I should go back to Texas where Doms..." Phoenix cut off her tirade when he landed a swat on her barely covered ass that he knew left fire behind because his damned palm felt like it had been kissed by the same flame. "Hey! What the hell?"

"Stop talking, *cher*." Mitch stood so close, she had to tilt her head back to look into his eyes. Phoenix was grateful his friend was taking the lead, because at the moment, he was much too close to the edge. Ever since their time in the private room had been cut short, things had spiraled out of control, and one of the things Phoenix prized above all others was being in control.

Seeing her eyes flash with annoyance when her mouth snapped shut in automatic response to Mitch's command, Phoenix felt some of his tension begin to slide away. Now that he'd taken a few deep breaths he could see her inflammatory words for what they'd really been—her own insecurities surfacing as concern for Coral. The few seconds Mitch bought him had been enough to get himself together, and he was grateful for his friend's insight.

With a short nod to Mitch, Phoenix grabbed her hand and headed toward the stairs leading to the basement…and their personal dungeon. Once their parents decided to move out, the Morgan brothers hadn't wasted any time converting one of the larger rooms on the lower level into a playroom for their BDSM activities. Calling it a dungeon was somewhat misleading because it was a high-end playroom by anyone's standards. The five of them had invested a lot of money in the equipment, and he'd never been happier with their decision. Suddenly the room seemed like a very good investment.

Chapter Eighteen

Aspen slid the tips of her fingers over the soft cotton sheets and let her mind drift in the haze between sleep and wakefulness. Stretching, she enjoyed the warmth of the sunlight warming her back and wondering how long Phoenix and Mitch would let her sleep. Without opening her eyes, she let her mind drift back over the events of the previous twenty-four hours.

Her first visit to Mountain Mastery as a submissive hadn't gone at all as she'd expected, that was for sure. Having her fantasy played out had been both thrilling and terrifying. Phoenix and Mitch kept things pretty true to what she'd originally written, and the few deviances were enough to keep things interesting.

She couldn't hold back her smile as she thought over their time in the private room, but obviously, that portion of the evening ended all too soon. From the moment they entered Master Nate's office, everything went downhill. Finding out she'd put an innocent woman in danger by coming to Montana had weighed more heavily on her mind than she'd realized...at least until Masters Mitch and Phoenix took her downstairs to the Morgans' playroom.

Rolling over, she felt the lingering effects of the paddling they'd given her when she'd refused to tell them why she'd been so angry in the truck. They'd pushed past her boundaries...no, they'd blasted through them. The two of them pushed her beyond anything she'd ever experienced before, not only sexually, but emotionally as well. The orgasms they'd given her eclipsed anything she'd dreamed possible, and she wasn't sure she'd ever be satisfied with vanilla sex again. But, it was the emotional release that shocked her the most.

Once the floodgates opened, she'd finally cried for everything she'd lost after being shot. She'd made the mistake of centering her entire identity on her career. When it was snatched away she'd floundered, not even her new job had been able to fill the void. If she was honest with herself, she'd known from the beginning the job she'd taken with DHS was simply something to fill the time.

When Mitch asked her why she'd refused Kyle West's job offer she'd cringed, but she'd answered honestly when she'd told him she'd worried about jeopardizing their friendship. Working for the Prairie Winds team would be a dream come true and even though she'd known she'd be able to fly again, her worries about working for friends prevented her from accepting the job. *Maybe it was time to reconsider that decision.*

Throwing aside the sheet, Aspen rolled to her feet and padded into the suite's enormous bathroom. The white marble floors and countertops reflected the morning light so brilliantly, she didn't bother turning on the lights. She smiled when she stepped into the largest shower she'd ever seen. The rest of the room might look like a high-end hotel, but the shower was clearly a nod to the outdoor splendor of Montana. The rock wall was laced with hidden LED lights accenting the spectacular colors layering the stones, and she wondered if Phoenix had laid the wall himself. Small ledges held ferns and small containers of flowering plants, the soft scents filling the air helped soothe her mind. Leaning her head back, Aspen let water sluice through her hair. Enjoying the pulse of the hot water massaging her sore muscles, she stood perfectly still for several long seconds before reaching for the shampoo.

"Allow me." Mitch's voice over her shoulder startled her so badly she shrieked before floundering. In her haste to escape, her feet slipped out from under her, but he caught her easily in his arms. "*Cher*, I'm sorry. I thought you heard me come in." She wasn't entirely sure he was sincere, but she'd barely been able to hear him over the pounding of her heart.

When she finally got her feet under her, Aspen turned to look into the steel blue eyes dancing with devilment. "You're not sorry. You did that on purpose." Stomping her foot in frustration, Aspen couldn't hold back her giggle at his failed attempt to look contrite.

"Never, *cher*. My years in the Special Forces taught me to be hyper-vigilant of my surroundings, and I often forget not everyone is as paranoid as I am." When she started to step away, he pulled her back into his arms and she gasped when she felt his erection pressing against her stomach. "I wanted to spend some time alone with you, baby." His large hands stroking up and down from the top of her ass to the base of her neck relaxed her in a way words alone wouldn't have been able to.

"Phoenix won't be angry?" One of the things she'd watched carefully with her friends in polyamorous relationships was the way the men seemed to work together seamlessly to meet their woman's needs.

She'd asked Tobi about it one night, and her feisty friend had assured her their efforts were far from seamless. "Even twins have communication challenges, but I'm rarely given even a glimpse of them. Honestly, I was really worried about it at first, too. I just couldn't imagine there wouldn't be a lot of jealousy issues. But, they seem to focus on what's best for me, leaving their egos out of the mix." Tobi had broken out into a fit of giggles before adding, "Who am I kidding? Most of the time, I hear them muttering about the fact they should have been triplets so there'd be three of them to keep me in line."

Mitch pressed a soft kiss to her forehead, bringing her back to the moment. "No, *mon cher*. Phoenix won't be upset. We'll spend time with you individually as well as together. I'll warn you now, we're going to be greedy. We'll take as much as you'll give us." This time, he kissed the tip of her nose before pressing his lips against hers in a kiss so hot she was sure he seared his name into her soul. Everything around her disappeared, nothing existed but the man branding her with his lips. When he finally broke the kiss, she was sure the world spun on its axis a time or two before the fog of desire abated enough for her to think.

"Phoenix and I have one point of focus—you. But I think you'll learn quickly our styles of dominance aren't exactly the same." She didn't say anything as he massaged the shampoo into her hair. The pressure of his fingers against her scalp made her moan, the decadent pleasure making her sway. He shifted to wedge her between his hard cock and the smooth glass along one side of the shower. "Like that, do you?" The teasing tone of his voice made her smile.

"I love having someone massage my scalp and face. I remember Lilly West picking me up from school one day when I was ill." Since Kent had been the one to walk me to the nurse's office, he'd encouraged her to call his mom instead of her foster mother. "I laid on their sofa with my head in her lap while she ran her fingers through my hair and traced her soft fingers over my face until I'd fallen asleep." Aspen hadn't felt a mother's touch in so long, at first, the intimacy had been unsettling. But in the end, Lilly West's patience won out, and Aspen had finally gotten the rest her body craved.

"Lilly is a treasure, even though I know she drives her husbands and sons to the very brink of sanity more often than not." Aspen tried not to laugh, but she couldn't hold back her smile. "I see by your beautiful smile you know exactly what I mean."

"And the irony is that they married a woman just like her."

"I'm afraid Tobi will be worse in the end because she's got Lilly as her mentor. I shudder to think what Kodi will be like, but I do know Kyle tells me he's getting gray hair just thinking about his daughter's teen years."

By the time he rinsed the conditioner from her hair, Aspen's body was beginning to hum with need. Mitch looked down at her, the fire in his eyes unmistakable. "If you keep looking at me with those fuck me eyes, I'm not going to be able to control myself." His words ignited her, and she pressed against him, relishing the feel of his rock hard chest. *Flesh covered steel.*

"Maybe I don't want you to control yourself. May I'd prefer you pinned me to the wall and fucked me until neither of us are sure our legs will hold us up." His answering growl made her inner minx dance a little jig in triumph. They'd discussed condoms last night, and she'd been glad when they'd readily agreed to forgo the latex. She didn't like the feel of it entering her and found they'd left her chafed and sore for days afterward.

Turning her so her back was pressed to a cool section of the glass. When she gasped, he chuckled. "I'm not sure

Phoenix intended for this section to be out of the reach of the warm spray, but I think it's a nice touch. His large hands cupped her breasts, gently tugging on her peaked nipples until she was squirming against him. He leaned down licking the shell of her ear and she wondered if she could come from this alone. When she shuddered, he chuckled. "You are stunning, and I'm looking forward to showing you all the wicked things I want to do to your delectable body. But right now, I'm going to give you exactly what you're wishing for. Hands on the wall, baby."

She didn't waste any time turning and getting into position. He smoothed his hands from her shoulders all the way down until he was squeezing her ass cheeks. The tips of his fingers lightly grazed the slick folds of her sex causing her to unconsciously part her legs. "That's it, open for your Dom. I love it when your body offers itself to me without your mind's direction—those are moves of the heart, and they are measures of trust."

Mitch's words unleashed something inside her, and her body shuddered with anticipation. Somewhere in the back of her mind, Aspen knew she was close to coming, but it hadn't fully registered before heat exploded in her core. The strength of her orgasm shocked her as brilliant sparkles of light danced behind her eyelids. Her knees shook for several seconds before they folded out from under her, but Mitch's large hands were already spanning her waist, so he easily kept her from sinking to the floor.

Aspen's head was still spinning from the intensity of her release, and the aftershocks were as intense as any orgasm she'd been able to achieve before meeting Mitch and Phoenix. "Again, *cher*. Give me another, come with me, now." His command was punctuated by hard thrusts, and the first spurts of his hot seed against her cervix sent her tumbling over the edge again. She heard him shouting her name as a woman's scream rent the air, but it took her several seconds to realize she'd been the one shouting.

"You're going to be the death of me, baby." Mitch's voice caught as he carried her from the shower, sitting her on a towel he'd already spread on the counter. Pulling another large bath sheet around her before drying himself, he told her to hold still and wait for him to return. *Is he kidding? I don't think I could lift my arms if I tried, let alone stand up. Hell, I may not be able to walk for a week.*

When he turned back to her, his eyes were sparkling, and she envied the fact he was able to move all of his extremities, and his mind seemed to be functioning as well. "Damn. I love that just fucked daze in your eyes. Knowing you're sated will always be one of the best feelings in the world." She wasn't sure what happened, but suddenly she felt as if a fissure in her self-control cracked wide open. Emotions she didn't even recognize started boiling over, and before she knew what was happening, she was sobbing.

"Fuck." Mitch's muttered curse only served to make her feel worse. Had she let him down? He didn't seem nearly as affected by what they'd just shared as she was. Maybe she'd been a crushing disappointment because he was walking and she couldn't even hold the towel closed in front of her. And now he was sure to think she was a blubbering idiot—*oh yeah, every man's dream woman, fuck 'em, and they fall apart. Dandy.*

MITCH COULDN'T BELIEVE he'd made such a newbie mistake. He knew how inexperienced Aspen was. He should have known better than to take his eyes and hands off her immediately after their scene. She'd looked so beautiful in her post-orgasmic stupor he'd completely forgotten to prepare for the adrenaline crash that had been sure to follow. She'd flinched when he'd cursed his own stupidity aloud, but he scooped her into his arms despite the look of apprehension in her blue eyes.

Moving into the sitting room of Phoenix's suite, he flipped on the gas fireplace and settled her on his lap. Pulling a soft cashmere throw around her, he smoothed the wet clumps of her hair away from her face. *"Cher,* I'm so sorry. I should have known better." She looked up at him and blinked in confusion. "I should have seen this crash coming, but I was too busy relishing the most powerful sexual experience of my life to pay attention. Well, that and in truth, it was taking a lot of my focus to keep from melting into the floor." It didn't make it excusable, but it was the truth.

"You...you liked it?" *Is she fucking serious?* Holy hell, she'd fried most of his synapses. He was damned lucky he could remember his own name.

"Oh, *mi amour.* Like doesn't even begin to cover it. You, my beautiful little sub, knocked me for a loop. Believe me, I'd have never let you down like that if I hadn't been completely decimated." If nothing else, he should have his ass kicked for not making sure she'd known how wonderful she'd made him feel. Seeing the insecurity in her eyes broke his heart.

Damn it, she deserved better, and he knew better. This was exactly why he'd always loved ménage scenes and envied his friends in poly-relationships. When one Dom dropped the ball, the other was there to pick up the slack. Vowing to do better the next time, he cuddled her against his chest and assured her their time together had shaken him as well. "There is a good and bad side of being more experienced in the lifestyle, baby. On one hand, I weathered the storm a little better simply because I was better prepared for it. But on the other hand, I damned well should have taken better care of you, and I hope like hell you'll forgive me for having my head in the clouds."

When she sat up bracketing his face with her dainty hands and looked into his eyes, Mitch's breath hitched. He'd never seen such raw emotion and her tears only added to the passion he could see so clearly. "I felt totaled. I'd read about the intensity of the emotional release, but I wasn't prepared the crashing wave of feelings." She smoothed her thumbs over his cheeks, and Mitch felt like his heart was going to burst out of his chest.

"And when I couldn't even move my arms, but you were walking and talking, I was worried it hadn't been as powerful for you. I didn't know how I was going to withstand your disappointment."

Mitch wasn't sure he'd ever felt like more of a schlep. It was time to retake control. She needed the reassurance his Dominance would give her, and he damned well wasn't going to let her down again. "Thank you for your honesty, *cher*. But the next time you are feeling insecure, I want you to speak up immediately. You'll never be punished for being honest. You will, however, be punished for lying, whether it's to yourself or either of your Doms."

"What's going on? And why does our lovely sub look like she's been through a tropical storm?" Aspen must have seen him enter the room because she hadn't seemed startled by his sudden appearance. Her giggle was music to his ears. Leave it to Phoenix to lighten the mood unintentionally.

Chapter Nineteen

Phoenix entered the suite just in time to hear Aspen shatter under Mitch's hand. Well, more accurately she'd been up against the glass wall of his shower as his friend fucked her into something resembling a wet noodle. They'd both been wrecked when he'd carried her from the shower, and then she'd crashed—*big time*.

From what he'd heard, Mitch knew he'd made a mistake and was setting them both back on the right track. This was one of the few points he and Mitch disagreed on, Phoenix didn't think their little goddess was going to capitulate so easily. She might be saying all the right things now, but Aspen had been on her own for a long time, and he didn't believe she would surrender that independence without waging an internal war.

In the vanilla world, Aspen's hands framing Mitch's face and her sweet words would have been perfect. But Phoenix knew she'd just taken charge of the scene, even if Mitch hadn't realized it. *His brain is still swimming in happy endorphins, lucky bastard.*

"Taking care of you is our priority, pet, and I think this clearly shows why it's going to take two of us to keep up with you." Holding out his hand, he continued, "Come. I'll try to tame your hair while your other Master recovers for a minute." She laid her small hand atop his outstretched palm, and he pulled her to her feet. He didn't plan to tell her where he'd gotten his hair brushing skills, most of the women he knew didn't appreciate the fact they were benefitting from his horse grooming experience. Taking care to carefully untangle the drying strands, it was several minutes before he could fashion her hair into a loose braid.

"Thank you. I was hoping to go for a run after breakfast, is there a trail nearby?" Phoenix wasn't surprised by her request; it was easy to see she kept herself in excellent physical condition. He didn't have the time this morning to accompany her, and he knew Mitch had work to catch up on as well. Thinking about her out alone on the running trail made him more than a little nervous.

"There is, but I've got a few conditions before you set out." They'd been walking to the kitchen, and suddenly he realized she'd stopped, leaving him to take several steps alone.

"Conditions?" Her arms were crossed over her chest and her brows drawn together as she scowled at him. *And here it is, that independent spirit we'll be dealing with.* "I didn't realize I was a prisoner. I was under the mistaken impression I was a guest, even though I was strong-armed into accepting the invitation." He shackled her wrist and tugged to get her walking again. Hopefully, she'd be more receptive to what he had to say after a cup of coffee and breakfast.

"Come on. I want to get you caffeinated and fed before we get any further into this discussion."

"So, you want to butter me up so I'll agree to whatever Neanderthal reasoning you're going to lay on me?" Coral's snort of laughter as they entered the kitchen reminded him why he'd agreed when his brother offered to remodel his and Brandt's suites. Combining the two would give him a large apartment complete with its own kitchen. With his parents using the small home he'd built at the back of the ranch's large homestead, Phoenix could use the extra space...and privacy.

Coral didn't react to his glare, but so far she wasn't adding anything to the discussion either. *Wise decision.* "If *butter up* is your editorialized version of *encourage to be reasonable,* then yes, that's exactly what I've got planned." He wasn't going to play word games; her safety was too important. Taking the plates, he'd prepared earlier, from the warming oven, Phoenix set them on the counter. She'd already found the coffee and watched him over the rim as he moved around to sit beside her.

"The trail is clearly marked and it's wide enough for two people to run side-by-side. My brothers and I cleared it several years ago, and we've also marked distance intervals which you'll see. It starts by the barn and wraps around the main property as a warm-up before winding up the mountain you see out those doors." He hadn't needed to gesture to the large French doors at the back of the kitchen because she was already looking outside, eyes wide with appreciation.

"You have a mountain running trail? Seriously? I may never leave." He knew she wasn't serious, but the thought appealed to him more than it should this early in their relationship. Turning to Coral, Aspen asked, "Do you have time for a run this morning? I'd love the company." Phoenix wasn't sure if she was genuinely interested in a running partner or if she was simply trying to appease him, but the look of horror on Coral's face made him laugh out loud.

"Seriously?" Coral waved at her stomach and hips. "Does this look like the body of a woman who spends any time running up and down a mountain?" Phoenix knew his sister-in-law was still trying to get back in shape after the girls' birth, but he also knew carving out time to work out in their home gym was damned difficult for her. "Thanks for the offer, but I happen to know how long it takes an ambulance to get up there, and Ryan wouldn't be thrilled with me for interrupting his morning with Joelle. He was the picture of patience while I was pregnant, but I'm sure I've already used up a lot of his good graces. I'm trying to lay low and rebuild the reserves before the girls get old enough for E.R. visits."

"They are Morgans. You'll be lucky if the local hospital doesn't give you your own entrance and punch card." His mom and dad still swore their five boys' escapades funded the emergency services expansion.

Coral rolled her eyes and grinned. "Don't I know it. They were reenacting their bedtime story last night when they were supposed to be sleeping." She shook her head before adding, "I still can't believe their father read *Five Little Monkeys Jumping on the Bed* to them. What the hell was he thinking?"

"He was thinking they were smart enough to see each of those monkeys got *hurt*." Turning his attention to Aspen, Sage shrugged as he leaned a hip against the counter. "Unfortunately, they seemed to have missed the point."

"We need to move them into separate bedrooms. Maybe then they wouldn't feed off each other. I swear they are manageable when they're alone."

Phoenix looked at Coral and laughed. "It won't matter. Our mom thought the same thing. Hell, dad built us all our own suites when we were kids hoping to stem the dares and competitions that usually led to late night visits to Doc's."

"It didn't work because my brothers steadfastly refused to admit I was faster and smarter." Phoenix groaned at Sage's comment, it was an ongoing argument. In many ways, the eldest Morgan brother had always been the responsible one, taking his responsibilities with his younger siblings far too seriously. But he was also prone to forgetting they'd all grown up—well, the jury was still out on Kip, but otherwise they were all full-grown men.

Mitch joined them and listened as Phoenix and Sage debated the wisdom of allowing Aspen to run the mountain trail alone. In his peripheral view, he could see Aspen becoming more and more exasperated, but it was Mitch who finally spoke up. "I think you two are underestimating her. Keep in mind this is a young woman who has flown dozens of missions over hostile territory without incident." When Phoenix started to speak, Mitch raised his hand holding him off. "The only time she's been hurt was in an effort to shield a woman she'd been hired to protect. Rather than having this become a point of contention, maybe we'd be better served by trying to minimize her risk."

Phoenix knew they'd be forced to concede eventually, but he'd also hoped to emphasize the dangers of being out on the trail alone. The stalker wasn't his only worry, wildlife was on the move at this time of the year, and the potential threat couldn't be ignored either.

Turning to Sage, Phoenix asked, "Who has permission to hunt on the mountain this year?" Sage was the only one authorized to give hunters the green light. They'd learned the hard way what a fiasco it could become if each brother gave permission to friends.

"Caila is the only one who'll be up there, and I'll send her a message letting her know Aspen will be using the trail. I doubt your paths will cross, she should already be in her stand, and I'll feel better knowing she'll be watching for you." Phoenix agreed. And knowing Caila was as good a shot as any military sniper gave him a measure of comfort as well.

"I'm not sure she'll be hunting after what happened last night, but it's probably a good idea to check." Phoenix watched his brother's brows knit together in concern.

"What's happened with the Mistress of Mayhem this time?" Sage had always been the most protective of the little girl who'd been born when he was just starting junior high school. He'd never complained when she tagged along. Hell, he'd often invited her when the rest of them would have happily snuck out without the little trouble magnet.

By the time Phoenix finished updating his brother on the what had taken place at the club the previous evening, Sage was pacing the length of the room like a caged tiger. "I'll kick his ass if he hurts her. And what the hell was Nate thinking letting her into the club?"

Phoenix rolled his eyes. "She's twenty-two, Sage. And from what I heard last night, she'd gotten a recommendation from another club. It seems our little star has been hiding her light under a basket." He almost laughed when Sage visibly paled.

"Don't. Just don't. I could go the rest of my life without thinking about this." He ran his hands through his hair making it stick up in the front. It was one of the gestures he'd inherited from their dad, and was one Phoenix bet they'd see a lot more often as the girls grew up.

Coral stepped up behind her husband and wrapped her arms around his waist. "I saw her truck speeding up the road a couple of hours ago. Kip was about five minutes behind her and judging from the way he slid to a stop out front, I'd say he wasn't in any better mood. Maybe you should text her and then check-in with Kip." Phoenix appreciated Coral's ability to calm Sage when he wasn't thinking clearly. It didn't happen often, but when his family or friends were involved, Sage could go off the rails as easy as any of them.

Mitch stepped out the back door to accept a call, and Phoenix watched as Sage sent a quick text to Caila. Waiting while he called Kip, Phoenix watched the light he'd seen in Aspen's eyes when they entered the kitchen dim as she listened to Sage rail at Kip for not protecting Caila at the club. *Damn it, Sage. Have a little consideration.* Since his brother didn't hold Aspen responsible, he hadn't considered the fact she might feel guilty for bringing trouble to their door. Before he could stop her, she'd slipped out of the room.

By the time he finished talking to Sage and made his way back to his suite, she was gone. Noting her suitcase looked like it had exploded all over the bed, he assumed she'd taken to the running trail. Hoping the run would help her process everything happening around her, Phoenix made his way back to his office. He'd tie up a couple of loose ends and then check on her.

Chapter Twenty

Aspen didn't remember ever needing a run as much as she needed this one. The weather was perfect...cool enough to keep from overheating and warm enough she hadn't needed a jacket. After a few stretches, she jogged to the barn and smiled at the precise distance and estimated times information the Morgans had posted by what she assumed was their starting line. Setting a decent pace, she ran the warm up track around the perimeter of what the sign referred to as the *yard*. Calling the area, she estimated at between thirty and forty acres, a *yard* seemed to be a fairly liberal application of the term, if you asked her.

Once she set out on the trail leading up the mountain, Aspen felt some of her earlier tension begin to drain away. She'd already felt responsible for their neighbor being assaulted, but seeing Sage's anger emphasized the point. Aspen assumed she'd already managed to lose his friendship before they'd even really gotten to know each other. Oh sure, she knew he wouldn't openly blame her, but that didn't mean his subconscious wouldn't always hold it against her. For months, she'd fantasized about how it would be to finally meet Phoenix Morgan and reunite with Mitch Ames. But the train wreck she'd experienced hadn't been anything like her fantasy...and hearing Sage yelling at Kip earlier hadn't helped.

It wasn't long until the trail became so steep she found herself needing to concentrate on each step. She was grateful for the distraction because thinking about last night's debacle wouldn't solve anything. The tree-lined trail was going to test her aerobic limits, but she was grateful for the burn in her lungs. *Keep moving, don't be a pansy-ass.* Her physical therapist's words echoed in her head and made her push harder than she probably should since her rehab had all taken place at sea level.

Making an effort to control her breathing, Aspen continued up the steep trail until she started to see black creeping in at the edges of her vision. Leaning against a tree, she gave in to the need to gasp in great gulps of oxygen until she started to become light-headed. "It's the altitude. You'll get used to it eventually." Aspen screamed and lurched forward.

Looking back, she saw Caila watching her, concern etched on her face. "Damn. That's one hell of a set of lungs you've got for a woman who was panting for breath a few seconds ago. Good recovery. Wish my patients could bounce back that quickly." *Patients?*

"Holy hand bells, you scared the shit out of me. Were you standing there all along? Damn, no wonder I missed you in all that camo."

Caila grinned. "Well, I try to avoid hot pink and orange when I'm hunting. Deer seem to be particularly averse to those colors, oddly enough."

Aspen laughed at the younger woman's sarcasm. The running shorts and shirt she wore were a psychedelic mix of swirling shades of pink and orange. One of the physical therapists she'd worked with had cursed her bland exercise attire and purchased several brightly colored sets for her. *Bright colors are motivating. Use any advantage you can, Aspen.*

The young woman's generosity had touched her and she'd promptly thrown out all of her drab workout clothing and replaced it with various obnoxiously bright combinations.

"Point taken, but the colors motivate me. Wearing something that deters wildlife from making me their afternoon snack is a side benefit." Aspen was still reeling from the scare she'd gotten. Having someone speak right behind her when she'd believed herself alone had rattled her. She definitely needed to be more aware of her surroundings. Dammit, she knew better than to become so lost in thought she wasn't cognizant of what was happening around her. Maybe she should consider spending a couple of weeks at Prairie Winds training with Kent and Kyle's team. *And what message would that send?*

Caila's eyes lit with laughter as she giggled. "Well, as strange as it may seem, considering the fact you've only seen me in black and camo, I love bright colors. All of my scrubs are bright, even though my patients don't seem to care one way or another."

"Patients?" Aspen didn't remember anyone mentioning what Caila did for a living, and now she was curious.

"I'm a vet. Well, more specifically I'm a veterinary reproductive specialist." Aspen knew she must have looked lost when Caila laughed. When Aspen started to apologize, Caila waved her off. "No worries. I actually get that response a lot. It means, while I'm trained to care for all animals, I specialize in reproduction issues, particularly those related to cattle and horses. I always wanted to move back home, and I was pretty sure I'd never be able to make enough money to buy my own spread by taking care of the pets in town."

"So you help infertile cows have babies?" Aspen felt like a dimwit asking questions, but she'd never met anyone claiming to be a reproductive specialist to cows and horses before. "Damn, I feel like such a city slicker."

Caila chuckled. "Well, not exactly. It's more about making sure all the cows in a herd *have* babies, and that they have them within a certain window of time. It's also about collecting and freezing bull sperm." Aspen felt her eyes widen in shock. "Damn, I'd love to have seen the picture that just went through your mind. But, whatever it was, the reality is probably worse."

"Think I'll just leave it there. My brain needs more oxygen before you tell me the gruesome details." The two of them shared a laugh before changing the subject.

"Did Phoenix sort out who is stalking the two of you, yet?" When Aspen shook her head, Caila rolled her eyes. "What's the hold up? The only other time I've known him to be baffled was when he couldn't identify you." Aspen found herself gaping at Caila, unsure what to say. "I play the games too, Athena. I'm Well-Bred Cowgirl."

"Seriously? Damn, you're a tough opponent. You've kicked my ass several times in Castle Charge."

"Yeah, but you smoked me in the flying games. That's how I figured out you were a pilot. I laughed when Phoenix and Mitch couldn't figure it out. And they're both Mensas...go figure." Aspen felt like she and Caila had a special connection because of what happened the night before. It might not be the best foundation for a friendship, but suddenly it didn't seem so important. Caila Cooper was remarkably easy to like.

"Obviously you didn't clue them in, so thank you for that. Mitch might have started putting two and two together if he'd gotten that piece of the puzzle."

Caila shrugged, but her eyes were suddenly downcast rather than sparkling with mischief like they had been earlier. "I think you give them too much credit. From my experience, men can be pretty clueless."

Aspen studied her for several seconds before speaking. "I assume you are talking about Kip Morgan." When Caila lifted her eyes, they were filled with something between embarrassment and pain. "He was definitely giving you mixed signals last night. But speaking as a woman whose three lifelong best friends are men, and who has worked almost exclusively with men in the Air Force, I can tell if you this. If you have to make a choice between believing their body language and their words, rely on what you *see*."

"Maybe, but it was hard to discount the brush off I got after...well, after we spent some time together." Oh yeah, Aspen knew exactly what *that* meant. The youngest Morgan had done a *touch and go*. The flight term referred to a training exercise where pilots take off, fly in a circle, touch down, then immediately take off again. But as with almost everything else, her fellow airmen had sexualized the term to suit their own needs. Aspen would bet the other branches of the military had their own version of the same thing. Oddly enough, most of the women she worked with were just as bad or worse when it came to their free and easy view of sex. Aspen had never been into one-night stands, and she felt sorry for Caila because she'd obviously read more into the evening than her partner had.

"I'm sorry it didn't work out the way you wanted it to. But I can tell you, he'll be answering to his brothers if he's hurt you."

The other woman's eyes shone with tears, but she valiantly held them back. "That will only make it worse. But, I'm sure you're right. I've probably made a mistake moving back home. I had several lucrative offers, but like a lovesick puppy I came home." Damn it, Aspen wanted to kick Kip's ass herself now. If he really wasn't interested, he should never have made love to Caila.

"Maybe you need to be the one who isn't interested. Men are just like women, sometimes they want what's most difficult to attain." The sparkle returned to Caila's eyes as she slowly nodded. Aspen wasn't sure she'd really helped, but she was glad to see the sadness lift from the younger woman's expression.

"I better get back to my run. Phoenix and Mitch are probably timing me."

Caila rolled her eyes and laughed. "I totally understand. They're an overprotective bunch. I don't know Mitch as well, of course, but from what I can tell, he fits right in with the Morgan brothers. My tree stand is about a half mile down the trail, I'll follow you, but I'm not running."

"What? You don't like to run? As slender as you are, I figured you for an athlete."

"Nope, I just work hard. Believe me, if you see me running, you'd better follow because something big and mean is chasing me." Caila shouldered her rifle and gave Aspen a mock salute.

Picking up her pace, Aspen made her way down the trail, admiring the markers clearly posted along the way. The men had done a great job with the trail, the steep incline was broken up with switchbacks making the whole thing challenging without being insurmountable. The real workout would come by increasing your speed...*and the damned altitude.*

BARRY ORMAN LISTENED to the women talk, the sound coming in loud and clear through his headset. The new listening device he used was still so new it hadn't even been released to the military yet. Scoring one before he left Washington, D.C. had been a stroke of luck. The new gadget allowed the user to hear everything being said within a mile in any direction, it was going to be a soldier's best friend.

Listening as the two women rattled on, he fought the urge to roll his eyes at their tedious chit-chat. *How can two women who just met last night share so much personal information?* He'd never mastered the finer points of chit-chat, quite frankly he'd never seen the point. Barry couldn't see the second woman clearly through the trees, but it was obvious from their conversation she was a local.

By the time the two women separated, he'd been close to nodding off. What the hell possessed them to chatter about shit nobody cared about anyway? Brushing his thoughts aside, Barry refocused his attention on Aspen Andrews as she ran toward him. Cursing under his breath, he knew he should have taken the time to get a more appropriate weapon, but the mess at Mountain Mastery last night had accelerated his timeline.

The small Beretta pistol in his hand didn't look particularly threatening, and it wasn't effective at any significant distance, but he hoped it would pack enough punch to render his prey immobile long enough for him to transport her out of the area. As soon as he gained Phoenix Morgan's compliance, he'd dispose of her body.

While he'd love to send Morgan bits and pieces, he'd decided it was too risky. Looking around him, he smiled. There were plenty of places nearby where he could stash her. Knowing she had to be getting close, he raised his small binoculars, bringing Aspen Andrews into focus as she rounded the corner on a switchback. She was nearing his position quickly, and he slid the mask over his face, adjusting it so his vision wasn't obscured and settled in to wait.

SAGE GLANCED AT his phone and smiled. He'd asked Caila to keep an eye out for Aspen, and evidently, the two women had spoken on the trail. *Located. Engaged. Watching.* The short text told him enough, and he leaned back against the warm leather of his office chair and wondered once again what the hell his youngest brother had been thinking last night.

Caila had been in love with Kip for as long as Sage could remember. The little girl with long braids shadowed all of the Morgan brothers, but Kip had always been the one she'd run to first. Unfortunately, he'd also been the least receptive. No doubt, the relentless teasing he'd been subjected to hadn't helped, but young boys rarely think about the long term consequences of their actions, and rest of the Morgan brothers had tormented Kip relentlessly about her crush.

Smiling to himself, he thought back to the first time he saw her after he'd left for college. He'd stopped by the local elementary school on some errand for his mom, and he'd spotted Caila out on the playground. Her pale blonde hair had been braided with pastel blue ribbons tied at the ends and she'd been sitting all alone crying. A wave of nostalgia overtook him as he remembered scooping her up into his arms and taking her inside. She couldn't have been more than seven or eight-years-old, and her tear-stained cheeks were flushed with embarrassment because he'd seen her crying. Her knee had been bleeding and her dress torn from a fall she'd taken from one of the pieces of playground equipment.

It had been the first time he'd called her Calamity, and she'd looked up at him, her big blue eyes clearing of their tears, indignation taking their place. "I'm not a clam, Sage. Clams live in the ocean. Montana doesn't have an ocean."

"You're right, sweetie, no oceans in Montana. But I called you *Calamity*, that means you've had an accident, well, it means you seem to have a lot of accidents."

"My daddy says I have them cuz I'm too venturous." No doubt her dad was trying to rein in her adventurous spirit, but something about the little mischief-maker made Sage doubt the local vet was going to have much luck.

"Well, I'm sure your daddy knows best, but if you ask me, being adventurous is a good thing. Think about how boring life would be without adventures." Sage chuckled to himself, remembering all the times that simple statement had come back to haunt him. For years, she'd justified her "adventures" by telling anyone who'd listen, Sage Morgan told her *adventures were good for her life.*

That adventurous spirit had landed Caila in a truckload of trouble over the years. Her mom had told him once she'd worried her daughter was trying to break the Morgan's record for the most emergency room visits. One summer, she'd fallen out of a tree behind their house and broken her ankle. It had been a fluke of luck, Colt was home between rodeos and saw a blur of pink tumble to the ground. When he'd found out her dad was in town, Colt had carried her to his truck and driven her to the hospital himself. Doc Cooper arrived a few minutes later, but Colt stayed until her leg had been set and the cast in place. Sage knew his brother had told her he wanted to be the first to sign the pretty pink cast, but everyone knew how worried he'd been about her.

Tapping in a quick message asking her to please keep an eye out for strangers in the area, he wondered where the hell the years had gone. He now had three beautiful little girls of his own, and he was scared to death they'd be as "adventurous" as Caila had been. *God dammit, I'll probably end up personally funding that damned addition to the hospital Ryan is pushing for.*

He'd replaced all of the floor to ceiling windows in his office and the master bedroom with impact resistant glass when Coral had been in danger. And, even though he appreciated the added security, he had to admit he missed the soothing sounds of the outdoors he'd grown up hearing. Sliding open one of the heavy panes, he closed his eyes and savored the brisk breeze.

The last days of Indian Summer were always among his favorites despite the fact it meant winter was just around the corner. The few songbirds who stuck around to brave the harsh winter would be spoiled with an abundance of seed compliments of his soft-hearted wife. He often teased her that he'd purchased the local hardware store to get a discount on the bags of seed she put out in an ever increasing number of bird feeders scattered around the ranch.

The breeze washed over him, cooled by the mountain behind the house. Grateful for the sound of the pine trees dancing in the sunshine, he wondered if they were enjoying one last celebration before the heavy burden of the coming winter snows. The sound of his office door opening caught his attention, but before he could turn to see who'd entered, another sound caught his attention. *What the fuck was that?*

Chapter Twenty-One

PHOENIX FINALLY NARROWED down the list of people who'd had previously unexposed secrets when he'd done their background searches, and only one of those had yet to be located. He and Mitch had come to Sage's office to tell him what they'd discovered, but an unmistakable sound greeted them before they'd even gotten through the door. "What the fuck? Was that a rifle shot?" Mitch hadn't even bothered to answer Phoenix's question, before running out the door of Sage's office.

The crack of a Caila's hunting rifle wasn't an unfamiliar sound, but the pop that proceeded it reminded Phoenix of a small firecracker. What the hell was she doing setting off fireworks in the woods? Just what they needed was a damned forest fire. He could see Mitch talking on his phone as he sprinted to the spot where the trail emerged from the trees and wondered who he'd called. For long seconds he was frozen in place, the reality of the situation slowly sinking in until the possibilities began to overwhelm him.

He heard Sage curse as he spoke on the phone and then felt his brother dragging him by the arm out the door. "Come on." Before they'd made their way to the barn, one of their side-by-sides roared out of the barn and turned to the mountain. Kip's face was a mask of fierce anger as he roared up the other end of the trail. "Fucking kid, we're going to have a serious discussion about priorities. Caila isn't the one in trouble."

They'd finally gotten to the other small four-wheel drive utility vehicle the ranch hands used because it served a multitude of uses, the thing was battered, but mechanically it was top notch. Phoenix held on as Sage drove the small side-by-side as fast as it would go over the rough terrain. He had to shout to be heard over the roar of the engine and the wind rushing past them, "Who's in trouble?"

"Aspen." Perhaps he'd been in denial—his mind refusing to process what was happening, but it all crystallized at that moment. It made perfect sense, Caila's rifle shot was in response to the first shot from what was probably a hand gun. The only thing anyone would *hunt* on the mountain with a hand gun was another person. Sage's one-word answer felt like a kick to the chest and he almost fell when his hand slipped from the roll-bar. As fast as they were going, they still hadn't caught up with Mitch. Hell, the man was damned fast, Phoenix would give him that. Sage must have been thinking the same thing because he muttered, "Ames is a fast fucker; I'll say that for him. And he was dialing the phone as he cleared the hedge behind the porch. None of us has ever been able to clear that thing. He went over it while dialing a phone like it was nothing. Fucking humbling, I tell you."

Sage wasn't ordinarily prone to chit-chat, so the fact he was making the effort to shout idle nonsense told Phoenix how worried he was. The only question was—what was he worried about? Aspen or the fact Phoenix was only holding on to his sanity by a thin thread. Fucking hell, it had taken him over a year to track her down, and now he could lose her after only spending one night together. *What the hell kind of justice is that?*

HEARING THE UNMISTAKABLE crack of a long-range rifle on the heels of the pop of a handgun as they entered Sage's office sent Mitch out the back door and over the hedge without pausing to answer Phoenix's question. He knew Aspen had to be nearing the end of the trail, and since the first gunshot came from his left, that was the direction he headed. He was already on the phone with Brandt before his feet hit the ground. The operative inside him knew it was important to get local law enforcement headed this way as soon as possible. He wanted to get EMS headed this way and Brandt need to seal the perimeter as quickly as possible.

If Phoenix was right about the perp, they were dealing with a man with access to a plethora of military grade equipment. If Barry Orman was planning to use Aspen in a plan against Phoenix, then he was planning to abduct her. Thinking about Aspen being exposed to the things he'd seen victims endure was Mitch's worst nightmare. The Morgans might know this mountain like the back of their hands, but Brandt and Ryan were the only ones trained to deal with a hostage rescue, and Mitch worried the three of them wouldn't be enough to get Aspen out safely.

The only sound he could hear was the pounding of his feet and his racing heart as he sprinted up the lower slope of the mountain. He was grateful the Wests insisted their team keep in top physical condition because he was barely breathing hard by the time he crossed into the trees. The sound of a motor tearing across the other side of the slope assured him the others were on their way.

The air under the cover of the forest was much cooler, and his first thought was how grateful he was because cooler air would slow bleeding. Somehow, he'd managed to shift from lover to operative, and Mitch was thankful for the emotional distance. He'd make better decisions if he didn't focus on the fact he was trying to rescue the woman who'd stolen his heart. Pulling out the weapon he'd tucked into the back of his jeans when they'd gone to find Sage, Mitch crouched and placed his steps silently on the leaf-covered earth.

Pausing every few feet to listen, Mitch was making slow progress when he heard another motor coming up the slope. Whoever was driving wasn't wasting any time, and he hoped like hell they had the good sense to stay outside the tree line, but he expected them to come in like gangbusters. The next time he stopped, Mitch heard the murmur of a man's voice, but he couldn't make out what he was saying.

Before he took another step, he pulled his phone from his pocket and sent a quick text to Phoenix warning him to stay as quiet as possible. He'd learned over the years, giving your armed enemy audio-confirmation of your location inevitably ended with them shooting at you. Suspecting they were already dealing with at least one victim, Mitch didn't see any reason to add to the list.

Before he took the next step Mitch froze, the distinctive sound of a woman cursing a blue-streak filled the air. Leaning a hand against a nearby tree, Mitch took a steadying breath. Christ, he was actually dizzy with relief at the sound of her voice. "I'm getting fucking tired of getting shot, you know. It hurts. People always say their bodies go numb with shock, but that's a crock of shit. It fucking hurts I tell you." He heard a thump followed by a low moan and would have bet his inheritance that Aspen had just kicked the man who'd shot her.

"Shut up, you pansy ass. You shot me, and Caila shot you, all's fair in love and war, you ass hat. The only reason she didn't splatter your brains all over the forest was because she liked my outfit. I'll bet she's a great shot, and she left you alive so I could kick the ever-loving shit out of you." Two loud thumps were followed by another deep moan.

Mitch was inching his way toward her, but since he didn't know whether or not she'd disarmed her assailant, he wasn't particularly inclined to startle her—another easy way he'd discovered a person could make themselves a target. "Don't even think about running, you idiot. You'll be lucky if you don't bleed to death before the ambulance arrives. And the closest doctor is a vet...and she's the one who shot you, so I wouldn't hold out much hope for help from that corner if I were you."

Smiling to himself, he knew she was chattering like a magpie to keep the fear at bay, but the adrenaline surging through her system was already beginning to fade, and he knew from experience she was about to crash. *"Cher*, it's Mitch. I'm going to come around the corner in five seconds. I'd appreciate it if you didn't shoot me."

Stepping into her line of sight, he felt his knees shake until they threatened to buckle out from under him. Aspen was leaning against a tree holding a small handgun with her left hand while cupping her left shoulder with her right. Blood covered her shirt, and her shorts were quickly becoming saturated. She was bleeding far more than she would have with a simple flesh wound.

Her eyes were wide and the palest green he'd ever seen; the wild look reflected in them told him Aspen knew she was badly hurt. He knew then, the act had been more about staying conscious than managing her fear. "Drop the weapon, *cher*. I've got you." She let the gun drop from her hand and collapsed into his arms.

The thump-thump of an incoming chopper was a welcome sound, and as soon as he stepped back onto the trail with Aspen cradled against his chest, Sage rushed past him. Over his shoulder, Mitch shouted, "Secure him and have the paramedics take care of him when they get here. And thank Caila for not killing him because Brandt's going to have a lot of questions for him." *Then it will be our turn.*

Phoenix looked completely shell-shocked when he pushed her blood smeared hair back from her face. Her eyes were closed, but she smiled. "I knew you'd come. I just had to stay awake until you got here." The fading whisper almost broke his heart, and from the shattered look on Phoenix's face, he also felt the sharp stabbing pains of guilt as they moved quickly toward the waiting helicopter.

Ryan Morgan was already running toward them as fast as his bent position allowed, shouting questions as they got closer. "How long ago? Was she conscious when you found her? Position?" It was the usual drill, but it felt profoundly different this time. This time, the wounded person lying limp in his arms was the woman he'd fallen in love with.

The time they'd spent chatting while playing the games Phoenix created had given all three of them a great deal of insight into how the others viewed the world in general. They may not have known her name, but they'd learned a lot about her. She'd told them how much she loved wildflowers and confided she slept best when soothed to sleep by the sound of rain. Mitch had teased her when she'd confessed to loving *The Three Stooges* and old *I Love Lucy* marathons.

He'd been reluctant to lay her on the gurney when they reached the helicopter, but Ryan's hand on his shoulder let him know the other man understood how important she was. "I'll take good care of her, I promise. But I can't do it unless you two move back. I want to assess her before we take off in case she needs something I can't do when I'm bouncing around. Lifting off from the base of a mountain can be a bitch, at least we aren't under enemy fire, but the wind currents are unpredictable. I need to take a look while we're sitting still."

Mitch nodded in agreement, but it was still damned difficult to let go and scoot back. Ryan quickly cut away her shirt and shorts before returning the snips to his pants pocket. The man had been a hell of a combat medic during his time as a Navy SEAL and Mitch found a measure of comfort in the fact there wasn't much Ryan Morgan hadn't already seen when it came to gunshot wounds.

Phoenix shifted in his seat, watching his cousin closely as his hands moved over Aspen's body. "Does he have to touch her everywhere?" The growl in his voice made Mitch smile.

"I'm pretty sure he knows what he's doing. He was one of the best combat medics in the Special Forces. Other teams requested him when they had joint missions with the SEALs, hell my own team nagged our commander to get him onboard several times.

"I didn't say he wasn't qualified. I said he doesn't need to touch her everywhere."

Ryan grinned and shook his head, "You're an idiot, cuz. I'm not discounting how lovely your woman is, but you know full well I only have eyes for my wife." Banging on the fuselage, he let the pilot know they were ready to go. Ryan continued working as Mitch felt the helicopter lift into the air. "I'm not thrilled about having to treat her at our local facility, but the flight time to a larger medical center is an even worse option. I've already gotten her medical records from Micah, so that will save a lot of time."

Mitch wasn't surprised the Prairie Winds team's computer guru had already hacked her records, the man was almost as good with computers as Phoenix. He also knew the Wests were still trying to recruit her, so they'd probably already built an impressive file on the former Air Force captain. There wasn't any reason she couldn't fly private aircraft and with her experience, she would be a huge asset to their team. This injury was definitely going to require extensive physical therapy, but it wouldn't be anything he and Phoenix weren't prepared to help her with.

By the time Aspen had been wheeled into the small medical center's trauma unit, Ryan had shifted from field medic to doctor, shouting orders and instructions as the door closed behind them. The silence, as he and Phoenix stared at the closed door, was deafening despite all the activity surrounding them. A young nurse led them to the nearest waiting room, but Mitch couldn't sit still. He pulled his phone from his pocket when it vibrated against his thigh and opened the message from Kyle West.

Back-up headed your way. Keep me posted.

Short and sweet, typical Kyle West. But his use of 'me' instead of us, let him know Kent was on whatever team was heading to Montana. They hadn't been leaving their wife's side, so Kent's willingness to make the trip spoke volumes about how much Aspen meant to them.

Phoenix answered his own phone, and Mitch assumed

he was updating Sage on Aspen's condition. He tuned out their conversation and tried to shut out everything else as he paced the length of the waiting room. *This damned room is too small to be cooped up in for very long. I'll go bat shit crazy in here when it fills up.* And it would certainly begin filling with friends and family soon enough.

The sudden shift in Phoenix's body language caught Mitch's attention, and he stopped to listen to his friend's end of the conversation. "How the fucking hell did that happen, Brandt?" Phoenix's body was practically vibrating with anger and Mitch dreaded what he knew must be bad news. "Well, they'd better find him just as fast as they lost him."

Phoenix ended the call and threw his phone against the wall. It exploded into a thousand pieces just as Coral stepped through the door. "Wow, bet that felt good." She grinned at her brother-in-law without an ounce of judgement in her eyes. "I can't even tell you how often I contemplate doing the same thing. I think our health insurance should cover it because it's as close to therapy as I have time for."

She never broke her stride as she walked straight into Phoenix's outstretched arms. Mitch envied his friend's tight family connections. He'd seen the Morgans take one another to task on occasion, but he'd never failed to see the love they shared. "How's she doing? Have you heard anything yet?" Coral's questions were muffled because they'd been spoken into Phoenix's chest, but Mitch heard the concern in her voice. Before either of them spoke, the door opened, and at least a dozen people spilled into the room. *Yes, indeed, this room is too fucking small.*

Chapter Twenty-Two

ASPEN WOKE TO the all too familiar beeping of medical equipment. Her mind was foggy and made her frown as she tried to sort out why she was back in the hospital. Hadn't she gotten out of CeCe's hospital? She remembered stepping outside into the sunshine after her friend finally agreed to release her from the small island clinic. The warmth of the sunshine on her face after being stuck inside for so long had been a welcome sensation. She'd stood still so long her friend CeCe had turned back into Dr. Cecelia Barnes and threatened to pull her right back inside if she didn't get moving.

Fighting to open her eyes proved too daunting a task, so Aspen listened for clues as to why she'd once again landed in a damned hospital. *I'm getting fucking tired of this shit.* When she didn't hear anything but the constant beeping of the monitors and soft hiss of oxygen, she stopped fighting and drifted back to sleep. There didn't seem to be any reason to force memories that were out of reach…quite frankly, it was just too much effort.

PHOENIX STOOD BY Aspen's bedside watching as she frowned in her sleep. At first, he'd thought she was finally coming out of the anesthesia, but the frown lines between her brows had faded, and she seemed to have settled once again, so he hadn't spoken. Ryan had been crystal clear in his warning, he wanted his patient to sleep as much as possible. "Sleep heals a lot of problems. I mean it when I say I'll kick your asses out of here if you don't let her sleep." The glare he'd given Phoenix and Mitch had assured them he wouldn't hesitate to follow through on the threat. The two of them had stayed by her bedside, only leaving to take a shower or grab a quick bite to eat. Bending down and pressing a soft kiss to her forehead, Phoenix stepped into the hall leaving Mitch to watch over her.

Leaning against the wall, he closed his eyes and sent up another prayer pleading for God's help. Hell, God was probably getting tired of hearing the same request, but he found comfort in the gesture. A warm hand on his forearm started him back to the moment. Opening his eyes, Phoenix was surprised to see his lovely sister-in-law Josie looking at him with worry in her ocean blue eyes. "Are you okay?" The voice the world knew as pop-sensation, Josephine Alta, was full of concern as she stepped into his arms. "We've already gotten an update on Aspen from Mitch, but right now it's you I'm worried about. Please tell me how you're doing."

At that moment, Phoenix felt overwhelmed with gratitude. He'd grown up in a wonderful family, and it was often easy to forget what a blessing he'd been given. But moments like this were poignant reminders of how lucky he was. Kissing the top of her out of control blonde curls, he smiled at the glare his brother, Colt sent his way. "I'm damned glad to see you, but sorry you had to put your vacation on hold. Sweetie, you really needed that break." Her recent tour had been insanely successful and she'd more than earned the month long stay she and Colt had planned in Hawaii.

"We'll still go. But not until we know your lady is on the mend, and you don't need us anymore."

"I'm always going to need my family, sweetness. But I'll agree that I don't usually need you as much as I have the past couple of days." It was hard to believe it had been almost forty-eight hours since he'd watched Mitch unravel Aspen in the shower. In some ways, those precious moments seemed so recent and in others, he'd swear it had been a lifetime since her cries of pleasure rocked him all the way to his soul.

Colt gently pulled his wife back so she was pressed against his chest. Wrapping his arms around her protectively, he leaned down to speak close to her ear. "Are you okay, beautiful?"

Phoenix wondered if she'd been ill, but pushed the thought aside when she answered. "I'm just tired. I'll be fine, though I think I might go find a nice soft chair somewhere."

Colt nodded and opened his arms. "I'll be right behind you." Once she'd disappeared down the hall, Colt turned to him. "What do you know about the guy who shot Aspen? Any clue where he's gone?"

"Since I did his background check, I know a lot about him. Hell, I even know what size shoes the crazy bastard wears. But I have no fucking clue where he's gone." He'd managed to retrieve the deleted file from his computer and forwarded it to Micah, but so far none of the man's known contacts had panned out. Orman's financial resources were also a huge concern.

Colt frowned before moving to his side. Leaning against the wall beside him, Colt sighed. "I don't know what the hell happened, but for what it's worth, Brandt is fit to be tied." Yeah, Phoenix knew his brother had been on a rampage since the neighboring county dropped the ball, letting Barry Orman slip through their fingers. Why they hadn't posted a guard inside the man's ground-floor room was a mystery to everybody. Colt grinned when he added, "And from what Sage told me, Kyle West has been making a lot of calls since he got the news. I can only imagine how those conversations are going."

Phoenix smiled for the first time in two days. "No shit. Pretty sure the sheriff and the deputy who was assigned to watch Orman are both going to be looking for work when the next election rolls around." He and Colt had always been close, and he appreciated his brother's effort to lighten his mood. Phoenix hadn't expected Colt and Josie to postpone their trip, but he had to admit, it was damned good to have them here.

"For the first time I can remember, I'm grateful the Mistress of Mayhem was in the thick of things. Sage told me she made one hell of a shot." The corners of Colt's mouth drew up in a smirk—his sarcasm wasn't wasted on Phoenix. Caila Cooper could probably outshoot most snipers. She simply never missed what she was aiming for.

"I'm glad she had the foresight to disable him, rather than killing him. Well, I was glad, before the jackasses in the next county let him walk."

Sighing, Colt nodded in understanding. "She's grown into an amazing young woman, and I think we've all forgotten she isn't the annoying little tag-along anymore."

"True. She certainly isn't a little girl anymore. I know this will shock you, but Sage seems to be taking this worse than any of us." They both laughed because their older brother was notorious for assuming his younger brothers still needed looking after.

"What happened between Caila and Kip? I thought Kip was going to blow a gasket when he saw her sneak in the back way a few minutes ago." Phoenix hadn't realized she'd been there until the nurse brought in a small bouquet from her and told him they'd been delivered personally.

"I'm not sure, but I know whatever it was has both of them running scared." Phoenix knew Colt wasn't going to let it go until he was convinced Kip wasn't going to pull his usual vanishing act. Kip Morgan had loved and left more women than his four older brothers combined. That wasn't to say he wasn't adored by each and every one of his former conquests because he was. But that routine wouldn't play out the same with Caila, she'd wanted Kip forever.

"If he breaks her heart I'm calling first dibs on kicking his ass." Since whatever happened started at the club the night they'd claimed Aspen, he felt like it was his right.

Colt snorted as he pushed away from the wall. "Yeah, well, let me know how that works out for you. You're going to be busy taking care of your woman, and I'm going to be busy tying mine to every available palm tree I can find for the next month, so we'll leave the ass-kicking to Sage and Brandt. Hell, they've already got the process down to a science, may as well let them handle it." Truer words were never spoken. Both Sage and Brandt took their responsibilities very seriously, while Colt's years on the rodeo circuit had left him with the cowboy saunter and easy-going attitude. Well, he was laid back unless it involved Josie, then his brother was wildly protective.

When Josephine Alta's former manager pushed the petite songstress to the point of physical and mental exhaustion, she'd run back to Pine Creek. She'd made a surprise appearance when her childhood best friend, Coral, married Sage. Colt had fallen hard, but she'd disappeared after they shared one night of what his brother described as *earth-moving passion*. When Josie reappeared in Coral's abandoned apartment months later, she'd been fleeing a stalker and completely spent. Colt hadn't given her another chance to run, hell, he'd barely let her out of his sight.

Before Colt could move away, Phoenix stopped him. "Take good care of your little subbie. The world needs more beautiful music." Josephine Alta might be the star, but Colt had a hell of a voice as well. "Damn, your kids are going to be so fucking talented."

For the first time in their lives, Phoenix watched as his brother's face flushed with embarrassment, but before he could question him, Mitch leaned out the door of Aspen's room and said the words he'd been waiting to hear. "She's awake."

BARRY ORMAN LEANED against the bathroom counter, groaning as a streak of white hot pain lanced his thigh. He was going to kill the bitch who'd shot him. Barry didn't remember much of Aspen Andrews annoying as hell rambling after he'd fallen to the ground, but he did remember her mentioning the nearest doctor being the vet who'd shot him, and how he shouldn't count on *her* helping him. Yeah, he was absolutely going to kill her. That damned town wasn't big enough for her to hide, after all, how many female vets could there be in fucking Pine Creek, Montana?

Thank God Deputy Barney Fife fancied himself some sort of Don Juan. The man had been so busy flirting with the nurses, he likely hadn't noticed Barry was gone before he was already miles down the road. Damn, he wished he could have stolen some of the narcotics locked behind the nurses' station, but that was the only place in the whole facility the deputy seemed intent on protecting. *Fucker.*

Looking around him, Barry wanted to rage at the mess Phoenix Morgan had gotten him into. If Morgan had just left good enough alone, none of this would have happened. Looking down at his leg, he shuddered thinking about the moment he felt the bullet searing into his flesh. He'd been certain the shot had taken his leg off it had hurt so much. The drug store he'd broken into earlier had been a treasure trove of goodies, and he looked down at the pills in his trembling hand willing them to numb the pain so he could get a few hours of sleep. Hobbling to the bed, he settled back and waited for the drugs to take effect.

It was a good thing he'd taken an extended leave of absence from work. Explaining how he'd been shot would have been damned difficult. At least, now he had time to come up with a plausible story, not that he'd need it after Morgan had admitted he'd fucked up the report. Hell, Barry would probably end up looking like a damned hero. Smiling, as he considered how that would play out was the last thought he had before slipping into a blissful, pain-free sleep.

Chapter Twenty-Three

ASPEN FELT HERSELF hovering just outside of consciousness. Damn, she hated feeling like she was stranded in a dense fog, unsure which direction to turn in her search for daylight. Warm hands grasp her cold one, the gesture reminded her of a similar moment in the small St. Maarten's clinic. But that time she hadn't been able to open her eyes no matter how hard she'd tried, she'd been unable to speak...unable to beg Mitch to not leave her side.

"Come back to me, *cher*. I can see you struggling. Wake up, love, let me see those beautiful green eyes. I promise, I'll be right here waiting." He hadn't been able to wait last time. She knew he'd been called away, but it didn't mean she hadn't wished things had gone differently. Their attraction had been almost palpable and she'd been thrilled to find out it hadn't diminished over time.

Fighting against the effects of the drugs took so much effort, Aspen was exhausted by the time her eyes finally flickered open. She appreciated the fact the lights were dimmed; bright lights would only slow her efforts to bring the world into focus. *"Cher,* I'm not sure I've ever been so grateful to see someone's eyes open."

His warm hand smoothed her hair back away from her face, but when she tried to turn into his touch, he stopped her. "Stay just as you are, love. Let me look at you for a minute. I don't want you to waste effort chasing a touch I'll always freely give you." Even in her diminished state of awareness, Aspen knew his words had a deeper meaning. "You belong to us, *cher*."

His words were so sweet she couldn't hold back the tears filling her eyes. Shaking his head when the first one breached her tenuous hold and slipped slowly into her hair, Mitch brushed away the damp track. "Don't cry, *mon cher*." When he let go of her hand, Aspen felt the tears gathering again. "I'll be right back. I want to tell Phoenix you're awake. He's talking to Colt out in the hallway."

It was only seconds before both men stood at the sides of her bed. Phoenix took her right hand in his and smiled down at her. "Welcome back, sweet goddess."

Embarrassed by her inability to speak, Aspen suddenly realized why she couldn't make any sound cross her lips. Removing her hand from his, she gestured toward the glass of water sitting nearby. Smiling, he held the straw to her lips, watching as she took several gulping drinks of the cool water. He smiled when he pulled the straw out of reach. "Let's don't overdo it, baby. We don't want you to be sick."

"No we don't. I'd be forced to kick your ass for making my patient ill." None of them had heard the door open, so Dr. Ryan Morgan's appearance startled her, making her wince as pain seared through her shoulder following the sudden movement. "Easy, sweetness. You're going to want to avoid those reflexive reactions for a day or two." She understood what he was saying, as a former soldier she'd been trained to control her reflexes, but it would be a challenge until the fog clouding her brain lifted.

Looking at the men flanking her bed, Ryan shook his head. "You're going to wear her out if you don't back off. Let me take a look at my patient. Go down the hall and check-in with the family. Let them know Aspen's awake…and chill for a few minutes. I'll let you know when I'm finished."

Phoenix pressed a kiss against her palm. "We won't be far if you need us, baby." She nodded, hoping her smile reached her eyes and he wouldn't see how unsure she was about their exit.

Mitch had been watching her carefully and she knew he'd seen the torment she was feeling. Leaning down he brushed a soft kiss over her dry lips before pulling a tube of lip balm from his pocket and smoothing it over the chafed skin. "We'll be right outside, *cher*. I'll watch the light above your door—if you need us, you only need press the button and we'll come straight away." Gently lifting her hand, he moved it closer to the call button. Aspen tried to smile at the frustrated looks on their faces and the muttered curses as both men moved out the door, but as soon as the door closed tears streamed down her face.

RYAN WASN'T SURPRISED when Aspen started to cry softly, hell, he'd been damned impressed she managed to smile when he knew her heart was breaking. Leaning closer, he grasped her hand in his and smiled. "It's okay, sweetie. The emotional reaction is one of the side effects of the meds you're getting in that lovely cocktail." Nodding to the bag suspended above her, he wanted to reassure her as well as let her know she would likely experience the same emotional overload for a few days after they'd discontinued the I.V.

"Consider the emotional roller coaster you'll be on for a few days a preview of early stage pregnancy. The medications are necessary, but they mimic the hormonal craziness most women experience when they first become pregnant."

She nodded slowly before saying, "I remember experiencing some of the same thing in St. Maarten, but this seems much more overwhelming."

"That's probably due to the fact we brought you out of the anesthesia sooner than Dr. Barnes would have been able to. The surgery she performed was more extensive and far more invasive. The wound you have now was serious, hell, you tried like hell to bleed out on me. But repairing an artery in an open wound isn't as traumatizing as being opened up. I've seen your records, sweetie, the equipment she had to use to open your chest was replaced years ago in most clinics. And I'll bet it's been replaced in hers now." He laughed and then felt guilty when she gasped after allowing a small giggle to escape.

"Damn, sorry about that. I'll try to rein in my sparkling personality until you're feeling better." He pulled out his penlight and checked her pupils with a light so bright she was sure he'd probably blinded her for life. Damn she hated those little lights. Grinning, he teased her, "I'll bet you're thinking about a few colorful ways you'd like to use that light on me, aren't you?" When she nodded, he laughed. "Yeah, I think I can take you, but there were times in the field when soldiers found a burst of adrenaline and knocked the lights right out my hands. I can't tell you how many of them were thrown against the nearest vertical surface."

All the time he'd been talking, Ryan had been checking her circulation and gently tugging back the edges of her bandage to look at the line of stitches decorating her upper arm. "Looks good. I don't even think you'll have much of a scar." Resealing the tape, he smiled at her, "Damn, I do good work. There won't be a reason in the world you won't be able to parade around the club naked as the day you were born."

When she rolled her eyes at him, Ryan grasped her chin and rubbed his thumb along the underside of her jaw. "Just a reminder, little goddess, rolling your eyes at a Dom is always a bad idea. There are some points of protocol we like to apply in every circumstance. Most, like this one, are related to being respectful to others." His entire face transformed when he grinned, "But others are just random B.S. so we have excuses to paddle lush asses whenever the whim strikes us."

"I'll bet you were a handful as a kid." She smiled at his laughter.

"You have no idea. The older I get, the more I adore my mother for not strangling me. I swear the woman should be nominated for sainthood. It's entirely likely the only reason I survived was because my parents made certain I spent most of my summers here in Montana with my cousins."

She knew his negligent shrug belied the affection he felt for his aunt and uncle. "Aunt Patsy treated me just like one of her own. She was tough, but fair. You always knew where you stood with her." He must have remembered she hadn't met Phoenix's parents yet, because he let his affection show when he assured her, "You'll love them both, I promise. They've been overjoyed to have daughters joining the family. Uncle Dean is an older version of Sage, though he's mellowed a lot since retiring. The same is true of my dad—thank God."

"If I hadn't done Phoenix's background check and spent so much time talking to him, I'd be lost in this conversation." Ryan suspected Aspen was a lot like his wife, Joelle. When she put her mind to something, she learned everything she could about it—every fact, detail, and nuance had to be read, processed, cataloged, and saved for future reference. Joelle had spent almost three weeks "researching" wood flooring when they'd remodeled their home. He and Brandt had been ready to tear their hair out by the time she stopped creating spreadsheets for comparisons and had made a decision.

"I'm sure you're right, lucky for me I recognized your tenacious spirit, so it was a given you'd already know who's who in the zoo."

"I'm impressed; I wouldn't have taken you for a Dr. Seuss fan."

This time, his laugh was full and completely genuine. "Don't forget, I'm an uncle to three very bright young ladies. We remodeled a bedroom in our home for them and quickly learned we needed a padlock on the playroom door. Little hellions wrote the book on divide and conquer, too. Keep that in mind when you get conned into babysitting." It was easy to hear affection in his voice, Aspen was the first to admit, she didn't know anything about kids, and the more she heard about the Morgan girls, the more leery she was becoming of spending any time with them.

"Now, back to business before your men come back in here like the Neanderthals they are. We'll be keeping you for a couple of days to be sure we're past the most critical points for infection. Then I'll release you into Mitch and Phoenix's care if you agree to stay at the ranch because I know you'll actually be safer there than you are here. There is only so much we can do here in the hospital without shutting down this whole wing."

He smiled down at her when her eyes began to slide

closed. "Damn, there is always a part of me that wants to whine when a female patient starts falling asleep on me. Never in my wildest dreams did I think I'd bore a woman to sleep." His words had been muttered more to himself than to her, and he fought the urge to soothe the lines of pain between her brows. Reaching over, he changed the dosage on her pain medication. Once she started moving around, it was going to take more to keep the pain at a manageable level.

After updating Phoenix and Mitch on Aspen's condition, Ryan tucked his hands in the pockets of his scrubs and headed down the hall. He'd planned to tackle the mountain of paperwork littering his desk, but after spending time with Aspen, he knew it could wait. There wasn't anything more important than spending some quality time with his sweet Joelle. Ryan already knew she was home and after a quick call to Brandt, their plans to surprise her were in place.

KIP COULDN'T REMEMBER the last time he'd been as pissed as he was at that moment. He'd seen Caila sneak in the back way with a bouquet of flowers. She spoke to a nurse, set the vase on the chest high counter surrounding the nurse's station, then left the same way she'd come in. *What the fuck?* She'd made no attempt to talk to anyone in the family despite the fact she had to know they were in the waiting room—the damned waiting room she would have walked right by if she'd come in through the front door.

To make matters worse, Sage and Colt had also seen Caila leave through the back exit. Rounding on Kip, Sage crossed his arms over his chest, giving Kip a glare that was impossible to misinterpret. "What did you do to Caila?" Since when did his brothers use her given name? They'd always called her Calamity and now all the sudden she was Caila to everybody. He hated it when the rules changed, and he was left off the notification list. And damned if it had been happening his entire life.

"I didn't do anything to her." Hell, he hadn't even seen her since minutes after Aspen was shot. And he didn't even want to think about the terror that clouded his vision as he'd raced to where he knew her favorite hunting stand was located. Glaring back at Sage, Kip was practically snarling, "She sneaks in and out of here, and somehow I'm responsible?"

Yeah, he probably was responsible or at least partially to blame, but it would be a cold day in hell when he admitted it to Sage. Once he'd found her leaning against a tree, her rifle still at her shoulder, it had taken him several seconds to talk her into handing the weapon to him. She'd been so focused on protecting Aspen, Kip doubted she'd even felt the weight despite her trembling muscles.

The limited edition Henry her dad bought her when she graduated from high school weighed almost ten pounds before she mounted the biggest damned scope she could fit on the beautiful gun. Hell, a conservative guess put the value of the weapon he'd pried out of her fingers, in excess of five grand. And it was damned heavy for a woman as petite as Caila to be carrying around.

Shaking off the image of the lighter weight weapons he'd buy her if she belonged to him, Kip reminded himself of all the reasons he should have continued to avoid claiming the little temptress living on the neighboring ranch. But memories of the passion Caila displayed during the scene they shared, still haunted him every damn night.

Kip had spent years barely managing to stay away from her because he'd been terrified of destroying their friendship. And he'd known how angry his brothers would be when things fell apart between them—and he'd known they would. Kip had never been able to maintain his interest in any woman for longer than a week, two at the most.

Pulling her into his arms on the mountainside and feeling her unravel at the realization of what she'd done, had forged a special bond between them. Knowing she'd trusted him enough to let go was one of the most humbling feelings he'd ever experienced. She could have easily killed the man who she'd seen shoot Aspen, but she'd made the split-second decision to disable him. Damn, she was fucking quick. She'd known from one heartbeat to the next, Brandt would want to question the suspect. "What if he's just the first one? I knew Brandt needed to know." Her stuttered explanation had been dead-on accurate.

But Pine Creek was a small town, and Kip knew Caila would have heard about Orman's escape. Was she feeling guilty about not taking him out? Had someone caused her to second guess her decision? Knowing she'd gone to so much trouble to avoid the waiting room grated on his nerves. Was she avoiding him or the entire Morgan family? *Fuck! This is why I don't do relationships. Too much damn uncertainty and drama. How the hell am I supposed to know what she's thinking?*

Sage laughed out loud and slapped him on the back. "You could ask her, you know." Kip stared at him in confusion. "Yeah, you said that out loud. Hell, every one of us talks to ourselves when it comes to the one woman who matters." *Great. Just fucking great.*

Chapter Twenty-Four

MITCH LEANED AGAINST the wall of the sitting room in Phoenix's suite watching as Kent West pushed his hand through his hair—*again*. He'd made the same gesture of frustration three times in the past sixty seconds, and Mitch knew his friend's patience was wearing dangerously thin. *Oh yeah, saying Kent is fed up would be a gross understatement.* Aspen's ability to rattle the West twin who had the well-earned reputation as the *calm one* was something to behold. Hell, there was only one other person who could make Kent curse like the sailor he'd once been—his beautiful wife. But then again, Tobi West might well cause the Pope let loose with a few colorful phrases.

Aspen's frustrated voice filled the air, "I don't know how else to explain this, Kent. I'm not a dim-wit...I know the job is perfect for me. Hell, it's my damned dream job. But your friendship means more than any job...it's just that simple." The sadness and resignation in her voice tore Mitch's heart in two, but he didn't move to comfort her.

Meeting Phoenix's gaze across the room, Mitch knew the other man was fighting the same battle. There was a fine line between providing the support Aspen needed and coddling her. *Fine line, hell. It's a fucking tight rope suspended over the Grand Canyon.* They wanted her to know they had her back while showing her they also respected her ability to deal with Kent. Holding back his smile, Mitch thought it was clear Kent was going to bring in back-up of his own.

Kent had been making the same offer since he stormed through the door of Aspen's hospital room five days ago. His pleas had gotten more adamant every day, but she hadn't budged. *Stubborn little wench.* Jax hadn't had any better luck and his muttered, "Christ, my sister is deaf, and she listens better than your woman," as he'd walked past Mitch had made him laugh. Of course, laughing had earned him a glare from Aspen which he'd happily added to her punishment tally.

They might not be able to paddle her just yet, but Mitch had learned the value of keeping a running list from the other Doms at Prairie Winds. By his calculation, if she continued at the current rate, she'd have one hundred and fifty-seven spankings coming by the time she passed the six-week mark. If her recovery was prolonged for any reason, the number could be significantly higher. Smiling to himself, he had to fight the urge to rub his hands together in happy anticipation.

"Fucking hell. Aspen, you are being unreasonable. You haven't been this much trouble since you started dating." Kent glanced at the door and his watch before returning his attention to Aspen. Obviously, the soft sell wasn't working, it was time to bring in the big gun. The West brothers were nothing if not predictable, and Mitch was betting Kyle West was probably already on his way. "Do you honestly think our friendship is so fragile it won't withstand a little turbulence now and then?" Mitch saw something close to regret flicker in Aspen's eyes for the first time since Kent arrived.

"I didn't say that..." She didn't get the chance to finish because the door opened and just as Mitch had expected, Kyle West stalked into the room with Tobi following closely on his heels. There was a reason Kyle was both hated and revered as a team leader. The man's demeanor was reserved on his best day and ice cold when challenged. When he entered a room, there was no question who was in charge. The West brothers might be equals in their business and personal lives, but they were experts at playing to their individual personal strengths.

Mitch watched as Aspen's eyes widened in surprise. And, he could have sworn she actually flinched before narrowing her eyes on Kent. "Really? You called Kyle and tattled on me?" Kent's answering shrug and grin had her clenching her fists in frustration.

"If you weren't being such a pain in the ass, he wouldn't have needed to call me, sweetness." Kyle's affection for Aspen was easy to hear, but the steel in his tone was unmistakable. Everybody in the room, including Aspen, knew the man wasn't going to take no for an answer. Now, it was simply a waiting game to see how long she'd keep arguing a lost cause.

Feeling the soft brush of fabric against his arm, Mitch turned to see Gracie standing next to him. "Oh shit, she's in for it now. I haven't seen Kyle look this determined since Tobi decided she didn't need his permission to go skydiving." At Mitch's raised brow she grinned. "Oh, did I forget to mention she was pregnant at the time?" When Mitch laughed, she grinned. "Oh yeah, that was an epic battle. He thinks he won, but we all know she was the one who walked away with the prize."

"What do you mean?" Mitch wasn't sure he was following the beautiful Latin-American beauty's logic. With her dark eyes and skin that always looked like she'd just returned from a tropical vacation, Gracie Drake-McDonald was a stunningly beautiful woman. But it was her big heart that drew people to her.

"I love Tobi; she is the sister of my heart. But there is a tiny piece of her that will always believe she doesn't deserve the two men who love her with everything in them. The damage from her father's abuse wasn't only physical, sometimes the worse scars are those etched into our souls. You may not see them, and they may not fester often, but every once in a while, Tobi needs the reassurance her husbands will love her even when she's impossible."

Gracie's lips quirked as she continued, "So occasionally, Tobi pushes them to the brink of sanity. I believe they understand her far better than they'll admit, but I'm not foolish enough to spoil it for them."

"Do you think Aspen is testing her friends? Is that what you're trying so tactfully to tell me?" Mitch already knew the answer, but the flash of relief in her eyes was all the confirmation he needed.

"You're a very astute man, Mitch. I can't imagine you needing any guidance from me. I was just making conversation." Gracie gasped as strong arms wrapped around her, pulling her back against Micah's chest.

"My love, there isn't a man in the world, let alone a Dom, who wouldn't see through that last statement. I don't know where you were leading this conversation, but I can assure you, Mitch knows full well when he's being led by the nose." Mitch chuckled at Micah's comment, and he'd bet his last nickel that Gracie led her husbands around more often than they knew.

BRANDT LEANED AGAINST Sage's desk, listening as the Park

Ranger for Glacier National Park detailed the circumstances of the remnants of the wrecked car they'd discovered earlier. The hair on the back of Brandt's neck was still standing on end despite the man's assurance the victim matched the description of Barry Orman, and his wallet had been found nearby. The burned car discovered deep in a ravine along a mountain road indicated Orman had been attempting to make his way undetected into Canada. "There wasn't much left of the body, that's for sure. We share a coroner with some of the neighboring jurisdictions, to be honest with you, most people driving these roads are smarter than this guy, so we don't have a lot of trouble. He had to have taken the curve at a really high rate of speed because the car launched quite a distance over the edge."

"The guy we're looking for has been stalking a government contractor, and he shot a DHS agent we believe he was planning to abduct. He has the resources to stage something like this to avoid being taken into custody, so I'd appreciate you doing everything you can to verify his identity." It didn't take them long to finish up the conversation, but Brandt wasn't convinced the accident was getting the attention it deserved. He had a great amount of respect for the Rangers in Glacier, but Brandt knew criminal forensics wasn't their area of expertise. And the winter storm headed their way certainly wasn't going to help. As far as they were concerned, it was a wrap.

"Have you told anyone else about this?" Sage leaned back in his chair studying Brandt carefully. In many ways, the two of them were a lot alike—they'd always taken their responsibilities more seriously than the others. Brandt often envied Colt's laid back style, but he'd learned a long time ago he wasn't comfortable walking away from situations if he could help.

"Yes, I've told Phoenix and Aspen about the accident. I left a message on Caila's phone, but she hasn't returned my call, which is unusual. I've heard she's in Texas checking out a job offer."

Sage's brows both lifted in surprise. "I thought she was planning to take over for her dad? Was she worried about Orman coming after her? Or does this have something to do with whatever the hell went down between her and Kip?" Brandt still didn't know all of the details of what happened between his youngest brother and the young woman they all cared about, but it didn't mean he wasn't still asking questions.

"I don't know. Aspen mentioned Caila was concerned we were going to give Kip a hard time. She felt that was only going to make the tension between them worse." Brandt understood Caila's first concern because they'd definitely given the youngest Morgan brother a full ration of shit about his flagrant disregard for Caila's feelings. The way he'd treated her after their encounter at the club hadn't set well with anyone."

"I don't like it. I don't like it at all. Fuck, Mom is going to be apocalyptic when she hears about this." Brandt agreed, but until he could talk to Caila himself, there wasn't much he could do. "In the meantime, I'll talk to Kip and make sure he understands the implications. Knowing she is considering making such a dramatic change doesn't sit well with me."

Brandt nodded before asking, "Do you know if her dad has told her he's sick?" The last Brant knew, Doc Cooper hadn't wanted to burden his daughter with the news, but the time was coming soon where the symptoms were going to be hard to conceal. He was already slipping. Hell, he'd been so confused earlier in the week he hadn't been able to find his truck outside the diner.

"I doubt it. I can't imagine Caila ever leaving if she knew. It's been just the two of them for a long time." Caila had lost her mother before she started high school. Several women in Pine Creek, including their own mother, had taken the young girl under their wing—making sure she learned all the things moms teach their daughters. Hell, Caila had more "moms" than anybody he knew. Those women were going to be lining up to kick Kip's ass if their "girl" didn't move home. *Fuck it. Just what I need a bunch of pissed off grannies railing on my brother.*

Sage chuckled. "I can see by the expression on your face you're starting to understand what a cluster fuck this is going to turn into if we don't figure out how to stop the damned snowball Kip pushed off the mountain. This is just one of the reasons I worried about the two of them ever giving in to their mutual attraction." Sage shook his head in frustration as he moved to stand in front of the windows.

Brandt let the statement go, despite the fact it surprised him. He needed to get back to town, there was more than enough paperwork piled on his desk to keep him busy until the end of his shift, and he had no intention of working late. He and Ryan had big plans for their lovely sub tonight, she'd been a handful this morning, and he was looking forward to spending a little time reminding her why snarky answers weren't in her best interest.

Most of the time, Joelle was the picture of perfection, rarely giving them any reason to punish her. Hell, they'd all been so busy, it had been almost a week since the three of them had even been home at the same time. *Maybe she feels like this is the only way she can get my attention?* The realization brought him up short. Hell, perhaps Kip wasn't the only one who'd let his submissive down?

On his way down the front steps, Brandt met Kyle and Tobi West. The look on the man's face foretold what was about to take place, and if he hadn't been on a mission of his own, he'd have turned around just to watch. He'd never known Kyle West to fail when he set his mind to something, his *take no prisoners* attitude was a part of SEAL folklore. He nodded to the couple and smiled as he watched Tobi scramble to keep up with her husband. Damn, the man was practically dragging her up the stairs. *Bet that was a fun plane ride.*

Chapter Twenty-Five

ASPEN FLINCHED WHEN she tried to fist her injured arm on her hip. Damn it, it just wasn't the same *don't fuck with me* pose when one arm was tucked protectively against her. It wasn't like she was the most intimidating woman on the planet, but damn it, at least she felt more powerful if she could face them down in what Jax called her pissed off Tinkerbell pose. Fighting back a smile at the memory of that particular confrontation, she re-centered her thoughts on the men standing in front of her.

"You think you can bully me into taking the job? Really? You guys are amazing." A grin flickered on Kent's face, and she wanted to roll her eyes.

"Well, *amazing* might be a bit over the top, doll. But, I for one, appreciate the sentiment." Oh yeah, she'd known exactly where his mind had gone.

"Oh good, Lord. Aspen, I'm begging you…don't feed their egos." When the three of them turned on Tobi, Aspen sucked in a deep breath of relief at having all their testosterone refocused elsewhere. She wanted to hug her friend for diverting their attention, even if the reprieve was going to be short-lived. Tobi's sly smile told Aspen she'd known exactly what she was doing.

"Pet, perhaps you and Gracie would like to go to the kitchen for something to drink. Maybe a nice snack as well since I know you didn't eat anything on the plane." Kyle's overly polite suggestion didn't fool Tobi, and it hadn't fooled Aspen either. The sparkle in Tobi's eyes made Aspen want to cheer, damn, the woman was fun.

Tobi nodded enthusiastically. "You know what? I could use a soda. And I'll bet we could make snacks for everyone, too. I've been dying to try a new recipe I saw on Pinterest."

Tobi had only taken a single step toward the door when all three men shouted, "No" at the same time.

When Tobi, Gracie, and Aspen all burst out laughing, Kyle turned to his brother with a look on his face making Aspen wonder if his head was going to start spinning on his shoulders. "I've been dealing with this for a week. It's your turn. The punishment tally is in the usual folder on our server." Returning his attention to Aspen, he added, "You've been dealing with this one, so I'll take over here." Much to her amazement, the room emptied quickly and in less than a minute she was alone with the one man she'd never been able to read.

Kyle West was a Master in more ways than one. He could mask his emotions better than anyone she'd ever known, so she was shocked when his expression softened, and he opened his arms to her. "Come here, baby." When she stepped forward, he enfolded her in his arms. The move unhinged her when she felt the first wave of unfiltered emotion crash over her. He'd sensed her need, and it had taken nothing more than a hug to unleash the torrent. His kiss pressed against the top of her head and whispered reassurances was all it took for the floodgates to open.

"Let it go, baby girl. I've got you—I'll always be ready to catch you. But I'm warning you, you're still accepting the job." She almost choked on the laughter bubbling up in the middle of her melt-down. They both knew she was going to give in. Hell, she'd never had a chance, but she'd needed this moment with him. Aspen had always been able to get around Kent and Jax, but Kyle had been a rock solid wall of pure stubborn male anytime they'd disagreed.

Aspen recognized the same traits in Mitch and Phoenix. She wasn't a fool, she knew it was a large part of the reason she'd been attracted to them in the beginning, but she'd also instinctively known they would be so much more than friends.

Jax, Kent, and Kyle would always be the brothers the Universe forgot to give her, but she'd fallen in love with the two men who'd spent almost a year coaxing her out of hiding. She knew there would be times she could talk her way around them, but there would always be a line she wouldn't be able to cross...and strange as it seemed, she found it comforting.

Pulling back, Kent smiled down at her as he shook his head. "We're going to have a long talk about the fact you didn't let your Masters know how much you needed this." She must have looked as surprised as she felt by his observation because he didn't miss a beat. "Do you think I don't know the role I've always played in the unusual friendship the four of us shared? That I don't see how important it's always been for you to know there was one person you couldn't get around. Even when we were all kids, I knew exactly what you needed from me. I think it's why I recognized it so quickly in Tobi. The two of you are a lot alike in many ways—don't think *that* hasn't kept me up many nights as I worried about what sort of mischief the two of you might get into."

Aspen wasn't sure how it could possibly work out, after all, the Prairie Winds team was based in Texas. When she said as much, Kyle's entire face lit up with his smile. "That's the question we've all been waiting to hear, baby.

We're working with Nate and Taz to set up a satellite base up here. We're outgrowing our facilities in Texas, so we knew we needed to branch out or relocate, and as you can imagine, Grandma Lilly vetoed the relocation idea in short order. *I'll bet she did. Lilly wouldn't let her grandbabies go without a fight.*

She heard the door open behind her and wasn't surprised when she was pulled gently out of Kyle's arms. "Your woman is downstairs scaring your brother with her threats to cook. She's done a fine job of distracting everybody so you'd have time to convince our lovely fiancé to accept your job offer." *Fiancé?*

"She has accepted, but I'd say from the surprised look on her face, you have some convincing of your own to do, so I'll leave you to it." Leaning down and kissing her on the cheek, Kyle whispered, "Don't fight this, baby girl. Give yourself this gift, you deserve it." Tucking his hands into his pockets, they watched Kyle saunter out of the room whistling *Let It Go*.

Mitch shook his head and laughed. "Who was that guy and what the hell did he do with Kyle West?"

Phoenix laughed and shook his head. "No clue, but it's scary how much he looks like Kyle. Damn."

Aspen couldn't believe it. The two of them were focused on Kyle and not explaining what the hell they'd meant by calling her their fiancé? Sometimes the audacity of the male species truly baffled her, but just as she opened her mouth to protest, Kyle's words replayed in her head. When they returned their attention to her, she could see the light of laughter in both men's expression. They'd been playing her, damn them.

Well, maybe it was time for her to play a little, too.

The End

Other Books by Avery Gale

The Morgan Brothers

Coral Hearts
Dancing with Deception
Caged Songbird

Knights of the Boardroom

Book One
Book Two
Book Three

The Wolf Pack Series

Mated Fated Magic
Tempted by Darkness

Masters of the Prairie Winds Club

Out of the Storm
Saving Grace
Jen's Journey
Bound Treasure
Punishing for Pleasure
Accidental Trifecta
Missionary Position

The ShadowDance Club

Katarina's Return
Jenna's Submission
Rissa's Recovery
Trace & Tori
Reborn as Bree
Red Clouds Dancing
Perfect Picture

Club Isola

Capturing Callie
Healing Holly
Claiming Abby

I would love to hear from you!

Website:
www.averygalebooks.com/index.html

Facebook:
www.facebook.com/avery.gale.3

Instagram:
avery.gale

Twitter:
@avery_gale

Made in the USA
San Bernardino, CA
24 June 2017